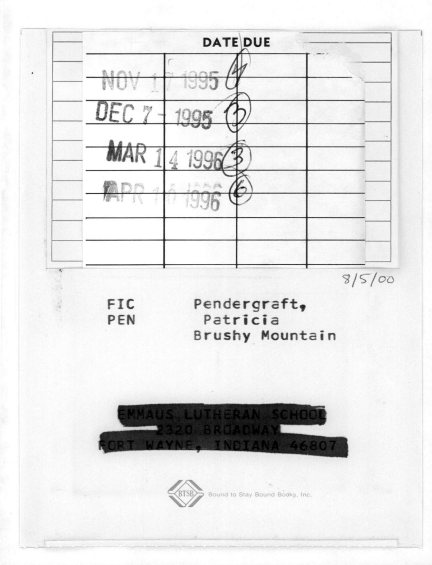

Brushy Mountain

Brushy Mountain

PATRICIA PENDERGRAFT

PHILOMEL BOOKS
New York

Library of Congress Cataloging-in-Publication Data
Pendergraft, Patricia. Brushy Mountain.
Summary: Arney wishes nothing more than to kill old
man Hooker who makes life miserable for everyone in
Weedpatch, but instead he saves the man's life three
times, leading to a slight softening of his character.
[1. Country life—Fiction] I. Title.
PZ7.P3735Br   1989   [Fic]   88-25431
ISBN 0-399-21610-3   First Impression

*This book is dedicated
with gratitude to my editor,*
PATRICIA LEE GAUCH,
because she believed in me.

"Brushy Mountain . . . Brushy Mountain . . .
What secret do you know? . . .
Brushy Mountain . . . Brushy Mountain . . .
I think about you wherever I go . . .
Brushy Mountain . . . Brushy Mountain . . .
Way up so high . . .
Will I learn your secret by and by? . . ."

                                Sal's song

Chapter
1

Old man Hooker come down the road slapping
and kicking his bare feet into the dust and grumbling like he always done, with his old tongue flapping to
beat sixty against his empty gums. Buck and Bill ran out to
meet him, jumping all around, barking and baring their
teeth like they'd come up on a snake. If they was anyone in
the world them two hounds hated, it was old man Hooker.
And for good reason too. Tice Hooker was the meanest,
nastiest, most no-goodest old hoot owl that ever walked
over the foothills of Brushy Mountain and along the roads
of Weedpatch! If a feller looked at him even crossways,
he'd near about slam his fist right into his belly, knock him
over backwards, and leave him laying right where he
landed! Seemed like everyone tiptoed around old man
Hooker except Ma. But Ma could thaw out the iced-over
creek in the middle of January with just a word.

Ma sure had a way with folks around Brushy Mountain.
I reckon they wasn't much of anything she couldn't do
once she had her mind tuned in to it. Ma was a midwife
and birthed so many young'uns into the world, she'd lost

count of just how many they was. Whenever they was a woman took sick, it was Ma who was called on to help out. She never got paid much money, but folks always give her plenty of food for us to eat and all the respect a human could ask for. Ma sure was a good woman. Everybody said that. Even old man Hooker, much as it must of hurt him to say a good word about anyone.

"Get them no good hounds off me before I kick their guts plum out of their hide!" old man Hooker yelled out furiously as he kicked at the hounds with his bare feet.

I jumped down off the porch and started shouting, "Buck! Bill! Come on now, boys! Come here!" I clapped my hands hard, but Buck and Bill just kept up a leaping growl at old man Hooker like they was going to tear his old dirty overalls right off of him.

I took off in a run out the gate and started kicking at them myself, trying to make them stop and go on about their business. It was too late, though. Buck already had old man Hooker's pant leg in his mouth and was pulling at it like it was a rattlesnake, and he was bound and determined it wasn't going to get away from him.

"Buck! Bill!" I shouted again and again.

Old man Hooker shot me a look like he could wallop the wind right out of me and yelled, "Get these durned hounds off me, you little devil!" His eyes was as big as Ma's washtub and his mouth was all filled up with the baddest cuss words a feller could ever hear.

"Come on! Buck! Bill!" I shouted, and I grabbed at Buck's big old flopping ears and tried to pull him away from old man Hooker, but Buck was so stubborn he wouldn't let go. Seemed like them old pants had to of been made out of steel not to of ripped by then.

10

Them hounds and me and old man Hooker was going around in circles, making a noise and kicking up the dust like we was caught up in a whirlwind, when all of a sudden there was a loud, earsplitting blast that tore up through the trees and across the fields and echoed back down. As sudden as that, Buck and Bill let go of old man Hooker's pant leg and looked like they was startled into being one of them petrified trees that you see up on Brushy Mountain. Then, as if they all at once come back to life, they took off in a wild run through the gate and around to the back of the house.

"Tie up them hounds, Arnold!"

I looked around and saw Ma standing on the porch with Pa's hunting rifle in her hands. There was a look on her face that said she meant business and I'd better be mighty swift about it too. I took off in a run around the house to get Buck and Bill tied up like Ma said to, and I heard her say, "Come on in the yard, Tice. Them hounds won't bother you no more."

Old man Hooker grunted and snorted and cussed as he started in the yard. "Goin' to kill me a dog or two one of these days!" he growled.

"You better never lay a hand on Buck and Bill . . ." I snarled under my breath as I heard the old man's feet hit the wood floor of the porch like he was stomping mad.

Ma had give old man Hooker an invite to the house for supper. And I didn't like that a bit. Ma was too kind to the old fool, if you asked me.

"Ma, why did you have to go and invite that old coyote to eat with us?" I'd asked her. I was thirteen years old and I aimed to have my say.

"The old feller is all alone now that Amelia is gone. Ain't right not to give him a good meal now and then," Ma had answered me as she'd spun around the kitchen getting the food ready.

Amelia was old man Hooker's only child. She got herself a husband as soon as she could and moved off to the city, and that left the old man to shift for hisself in that shack of his at the foot of Brushy Mountain. Folks said it was a good thing Amelia got away from him because he was about as cussed mean to her as he was to everyone else. I heard tell how once he took a stick to Amelia and walloped her all the way to the schoolhouse when she complained that she was sick. And once he made her go out looking for his old milk cow that was always wandering off, right in the middle of a winter storm. He never allowed her to have no boyfriends ner to go to dances ner any of the things the other girls got to do. I reckon that's one reason she took off with Edward Martin and married him as fast as she did. Old man Hooker probably would of went hunting for Edward Martin, but word reached Weedpatch that he'd been called up to go into the Army.

Once old man Hooker knocked Mr. Doogle, who runs the Cash-and-Carry store in town, right up against a shelf of canned goods and sent the canned goods tumbling every which way. All Mr. Doogle had done was to tell Tice Hooker that he ought not to of treated Amelia so bad that she took off and got hitched. But that ain't the worst of it. That old sidewinder threw Granny Stallcup out of that shack she rented from him for close to ten some odd years because she had got behind on her rent payments. If Ma hadn't took her in and let her stay in our storage room, no telling what would of happened to Granny.

Well, you can see what I mean when I tell you old man Hooker was the meanest man in nine counties. I reckon, if the truth was known, there ain't never been a meaner man nowhere. If they was giving out prizes for meanness, he'd walk away with the first prize every time.

Chapter
2

After I got the hounds tied up in the backyard I went and set down on the edge of the porch and started swinging my legs back and forth. It was a lazy, leg-swinging day, seeing as how I didn't go to school that morning, and all I done was wander around with my sore throat that seemed to get well before the sun come out good. Ma said I must of decided to play possum since my complaining stopped soon as it was too late to walk the mile down the road to school. But she allowed that by the time I'd get there, it would be time to turn around and start home.

The porch and house was built high off the ground on wood stilts and you could see all the way under the house and out the other side, if you bent down. Ma kept some home canned fruits and vegetables under there because it was cool. The chickens took to roosting under there and, heck, inside the house, the floorboards was so far apart you could watch them chickens walking around and cackling all day long, if you didn't have nothing better to do. In the winter, we stuck papers in the cracks to keep the inside of the house warm. I reckon we was as poor as church mice, all right.

My pa had went off to the war soon as it started up and he never did come back home. One day Ma got an important letter that was brought out to the house by Mr. Sage Johnson, the mail carrier. He got out of his Model T and come up to the house so slow and hang-dog looking that Ma knowed right away something was wrong. Soon as she walked out on the porch and seen the letter in Mr. Johnson's hand, her whole face changed. It took on a hard look like it was carved right out of one of them big boulders up on Brushy Mountain. Me and Sal, my two-year-younger sister, watched like old Buck and Bill when they've got a bead on a quail down by the creek, with our ears standing up and our eyes not blinking, while Ma took the letter from Mr. Johnson.

"I'm mighty sorry, Miz Burdette," Mr. Johnson said with his eyes looking down at the tops of his shoes.

Ma opened the envelope and read the letter with her lips moving like they always do when she reads to herself. Her dark eyes seemed to grow even darker with what she read, and a wisp of her dark hair fell onto her forehead. Her lips stopped moving while she blew the hair away. Then she read a little more, sighed wearily, looked back up at Mr. Johnson and said, "Well, I reckon I ain't the only one who got a letter like this?" It was a question and Mr. Johnson answered with, "No, Ma'am, you ain't. Miz Becker down the road and Miz Pine in town, they both got letters like yourn."

"Miz Becker? Miz Pine?" Ma's face turned white and pained. Me and Sal shot a quick look at each other. When we looked back, Mr. Johnson was running his hand under his nose.

"Yes'um," he said. "Albert Becker and the Pine boy, they won't never be coming back to Weedpatch no more." Mr. Johnson pulled a big blue handkerchief out of his back pocket and blowed his nose into it.

Ma's chin commenced to quiver like she was going to cry, but she didn't. She glanced over at me and Sal and took in another big, deep breath, raised her shoulders back and looked as tall and full of strength as she always did. "Tell Miz Becker and Miz Pine I'll be along to see them right soon," Ma told Mr. Johnson.

"Yes'um, I'll do that," Mr. Johnson said, and he sent a look over to me and Sal like the sight of us two near about killed him. Then he left the porch and hurried to get into his Model T and drove off down the road.

That's how we come to know Pa was killed in the war with Hitler. That night me and Sal slept on a pallet on the floor in Ma's bedroom. Deep in the night when Ma had fell asleep and the light from the moon was playing over me and Sal and the sound of the branches from the pepper tree was brushing against the house in a slow, swaying movement, Sal whispered, "You asleep, Arney?"

"No, I'm awake," I whispered back.

"I hate Hitler!"

"Me too."

"You reckon them Germans give our Pa a funeral, Arney?"

"No," I said, and my heart was so heavy it seemed like I could feel it bearing down on my whole insides. If a heart could drop and fall all the way through a feller, I reckon that's the way I felt. I had to turn my face into my piller so Sal wouldn't know I was tore to pieces and crying inside like I'd never stop.

"They ought to of give Pa a nice funeral and sung him some German hymns," Sal went on, and her voice sounded like she could hardly get the words out. Maybe she was crying inside too, I thought. I didn't have the heart to tell her Pa was probably plowed under right where he was killed.

"Go to sleep now, Sally." Suddenly Ma's voice was in the room and Sal was crying and throwing back the covers from the pallet and jumping up on Ma's bed. "Hush now, Sally. Ain't no need to cry for your Pa this way. He's where he can't be hurt no more," Ma went on soothingly to Sal.

"N-not even by t-the Germans?" Sal asked with a struggle.

"Most especially not by the Germans," Ma answered fiercely.

I turned my head and looked out the thin curtains through the winder. Brushy Mountain loomed up like a giant's belly after a big meal. The moon cast a bright glow over the foothills and made the little bushes and stumpy trees look like small figures on the giant's shirt. Sometimes at night I'd lay in bed in my own room and stare out the winder and see the mountain peering down over the town and them figures making a deep black shadder in the moonlight, and I'd get the shivers and have to duck my head under the covers. Them times I'd go to thinking about the stories I'd heard about the wolves that run in a pack up there and I'd think I could hear them right outside my winder. Then I'd go to thinking about Pa and wondering why he had to end up all the way across the world from Weedpatch and be killed in a strange country. Then I'd go to thinking about how Pa had run the filling station before he was called off to war. When Vesper Gene DeGoff took over for him, Pa told him he'd be back soon as he whupped old Hitler. I reckon him ner Vesper Gene, neither one, thought he'd never be coming back to run the filling station. Fact of the matter is, I never thought he wouldn't come back, neither.

I better explain right now that Weedpatch is the name of our town. Pa said it was named that because when folks first settled here, the land wasn't nothing but a patch of weeds. Me and Pa laughed about it a lot. He said they didn't have much imagination to of named it that.

Folks in Weedpatch loved Pa. He was always there to help out anyone in need. He helped Lessie Fay Harmon add on rooms to her house after her husband died so she could make it into a boarding house. He helped get a wood stove for the school, made signs for the post office and the feed store and built the steeple on the church so tall that you can see it first thing when you come into town. I reckon I'll never forget the way Pa looked when that steeple was finished. Like he'd done the biggest thing he could ever do. But the truth was, the biggest thing he could ever do was to die for his country. And that's what he done.

It was along about this time that Ma went to birthing babies and taking in sewing to help out, and things that needed fixing around the place didn't get fixed too often and me and Sal went to wearing more patches on our clothes than we ever done before. Some of the kids in school started in to teasing us for our wore-out clothes and run-down shoes. We wasn't the only ones being teased but Sal, being a girl and all, took it pretty hard. Just about every day or two she come home complaining to Ma about the old clothes she had to wear and about Daphne Hazelton calling her names. Ma sewed for Miz Hazelton and Miz Hazelton was always having her make pretty dresses for Daphne. I could always tell when Ma was working on a dress for Daphne. Sal would get a look of pure hunger on her face and couldn't seem to stay away from the fabric. She would run her fingers over it and touch it to her cheeks, and Ma would have to tell her to put it down so she could work on it. Seemed like it was harder for Sal to be a girl in them days, wearing patches and never having a decent dress, than it was for me to be a boy.

Well, them was all the things I would think about with my head under my covers.

But, to get back to that night in Ma's bedroom when we first heard about Pa, Sal must have fell asleep right away after she climbed up in Ma's bed. I could hear her breathing in that heavy way she has when she's sleeping and, after a little while, the bed springs made a squeaky sound when Ma turned over.

I sighed and tried to close my eyes but I just kept staring out the winder at the mountain.

"Brushy Mountain . . . Brushy Mountain . . . what secret do you know . . .?" I whispered to the mountain.

"Did you say something, Arnold?" Ma's voice startled me.

"No, Ma," I answered her.

19

"Arnold?"

"What, Ma?"

"Do you want to cry?"

"No, Ma," I said in a firm voice that hid my tears behind it.

"Well, if you want to, don't hold back. It's just you and me awake."

"I know, Ma."

"Arnold," she said after a few minutes, "always strive to be as good as your Pa was."

"I will, Ma," I promised her. But as time went on, I didn't know if I could keep on with my promise, I come to hate that no good Tice Hooker so much.

Chapter
3

While I was sitting there on the porch swinging my legs and thinking my thoughts about the time Pa died and all and gandering at the chickens and old Buck and Bill sniffing at the ground, Sal come walking up from the back field. She was wearing a right nice dress that Ma made out of some print flour sacks and some shoes that was give to her, and her blond hair was curled up tight and close to her head. It was always tight and kinky-looking the first day after she took the curlers out. Later on it would shake out and sway around her head in soft-looking fluffs. Sal was pretty but she was always ashamed of the way she looked. Mostly because of the clothes she had to wear.

I could tell right off that Sal was upset about something more than her clothes, though. Her mouth was all squeezed up and her chin was twitching. When she got closer, I could see her eyes was spitting fire, like she was madder than all get out. She come into the yard and yelled angrily at Gobble, who had just come flying around the corner of the house. Gobble was our one and only tom turkey, give to Ma by Mr. Charley Parlier for birthing his first-born son on Thanksgiving Eve. Mr. Parlier told Ma to kill Gobble and have him for our Thanksgiving dinner, but me and Sal put up such a fuss that Ma didn't have the heart to kill that turkey. Me and Sal would of ruther et dirt than see that big beautiful tom killed and setting on our supper table.

Ma let us have our way and from then on Gobble was just like a pet to us. Me and Sal sometimes run races with him. We'd start at the front of the house and run a circle around it. Gobble would win every time. And he'd foller us all around like some old friend. Thing was, though, he was so big and growed up so fast that, half the time, he was in everybody's way, running around the yard underfoot, standing in the way of the front door when someone wanted to go inside the house and just generally making a pest of hisself. Still, he was almost as important to us as Buck and Bill, and Sal wouldn't of yelled at him if she'd felt her normal self.

Gobble jumped and flew across the yard when Sal yelled at him and went to making that high, shrill GOBBB-LLLLEEE noise. When Sal got closer, I could see she had tears in her eyes.

"Someone been teasing you again?" I asked her. She looked up and seen me and mashed her lips down hard against each other and sighed a big windy sigh.

"Gussie Bilbow called me 'old flour sack' and I punched him right in his big fat belly!" Sal muttered.

"Good girl!" I said. "Ain't no reason to act so awful about it. You ought to be feeling good that you got a lick in."

Sal come and scooted up on the porch beside me and

went to swinging her legs right along with mine. "I punched Travis Satterfield in his nose and it started bleeding," Sal said as she looked out over the yard.

"You had to fight *both* of them?"

"I reckon I did," Sal said with another big sigh.

"What did Miz Tinker do?"

Sal turned and looked at me. "She grabbed my arm and slung me away." There was a bitter sting in her voice and a pained look on her face. Her gray-blue eyes filled with even more tears.

"She ought not to of laid a hand on you! She knows how them two is always on to you! She ought to of done something to Gussie and Travis," I said with anger beating inside me. It wasn't fair that Miz Tinker should take their side.

Sal's chin shook even more than it had before. "Teacher thinks I'm just an old bag of rags!"

"No, she don't, Sal."

"Yes, she does, Arney! If I had pretty, new clothes like Daphne Hazelton has, she'd think better of me."

My heart ached to hear Sal talk that way, but before I could say anything, she hurried on.

"And not only that! Old man Hooker chased me right out of the cemetery this morning when I passed through it, taking the shortcut to school. I run so fast I stumbled right over old Benny Pool's gravestone!"

My mind turned to thunder! I could feel my heart slapping like a thick, hot rag again and again against the inside of my chest. Old man Hooker again! I stared at Sal. I hated to tell her Ma had invited that mean old thing to eat supper with us and that he was inside the house right then.

Sal turned and looked right into my eyes. Even in her

pain, her face was pert looking. She always had a smart look about her. She could draw and sing like a pure songbird too. She could make up a song and sing it quicker than you could count ten.

"What was you doing for him to chase you?" I asked. But I knowed it didn't take a thing much for old man Hooker to start in on someone.

"I was only passing through the cemetery just like everyone does when they don't want to be late for school. I stopped to pick up the prettiest leaf, Arney. It looked like it was left over from last fall. It had red and yeller and rusty colors and, well I picked it up and was thinking on taking it to school with me and tracing it on paper when Tice Hooker jumped out at me from nowhere, it seemed like. He slapped the leaf out of my hand and yelled, 'You young'uns is always disturbing the dead! Let 'em be!' I was too surprised to say anything and when I didn't, he took off right at me! I never run from no one so fast in my life!"

I knowed that old man Hooker's dead wife was buried in the cemetery but that didn't give him no right to chase Sal and to scare her like he done.

I turned my head and looked back at the house with my eyes narrowed, mad as a hornet that Ma could be giving old man Hooker supper when he was so all-out no good. I looked back at Sal. She was staring at the ground, her teeth bit hard into her lip. It didn't seem fair that a nice girl like Sal had to be treated so bad.

Something had to be done about old man Hooker. What it was, I wasn't sure yet. But I knowed it would come to me. All I needed was a little time to think on it.

Chapter

4

After a little while, Ma called me and Sal in for supper, and when we went into the house to wash up at the kitchen sink we seen old man Hooker setting at the table like he owned the place. He had a sour, plumb-nasty look on his old wrinkled, sun-battered face. His eyebrows come together in the middle like an old beetle bug and he had little mean-looking eyes and a mouth that was so long and narrow, it looked like a string. His hands was sun-battered too, and bony, with long, knobby fingers and chipped-off, dirty nails. His whole body was so skinny-scrawny looking that it appeared like a small breeze could blow him over, but the truth was, he could fight like a tornado when he was riled up.

I waited for Sal to wash her hands, then I washed mine and we went to our places at the table and sat down.

"Where's Granny?" I asked Ma.

"Granny is resting in her room," Ma answered as she brought a pan of still-bubbling, white-flour gravy to the table and poured it into a bowl.

When Ma sat down, I asked, "Ain't Granny going to eat?"

"No," Ma answered with a solemn look on her face.

"Humph!" Old man Hooker snorted.

It seemed to take the brightness right out of the kitchen to have that old man setting at the table, scowling over us like we wasn't good enough to set at our own table with him. I glanced around at the pretty pot holders on the wall behind the stove and at the bowls of purple and white petunias on the winder sill and wondered how Ma could set at the same table with him after him throwing Granny Stallcup out of her little house the way he done. Weedpatch was small and folks generally shared what they could, but having to share our food with the likes of Tice Hooker was like seeing a nightmare come alive. I half expected to see them petunias on the winder sill to wilt dead away!

"We'll have grace now, Arnold," Ma said, and I said it even though I didn't want to. Not with Tice Hooker setting there hawking over the vittles the way he was.

While I was saying the grace, I glanced over at Sal. She was looking down at her plate like she'd been betrayed by Ma by allowing Tice Hooker to be there. Then I glanced at him. His head wasn't even down. He had picked up a biscuit and was setting there munching on it like he didn't have to thank the Lord for nothing he et. It sure got off with me how one human being could be so low down.

Ma raised her head when I finished saying the grace and said, "Thank you, Arnold. That was right nice." Then she went to passing all the food to old man Hooker first, while me and Sal just sat there and watched.

Sal punched my leg under the table when old man

26

Hooker took *two* steaming roastin'ears off the platter, leaving only one. He had already et half the pan of biscuits by the time they got to me and he sloshed the gravy and pertaters out of the bowls into his plate like they was all, every last bit, meant for him! When I took the platter with the one roastin'ear on it I passed it on to Sal. She shook her head, meaning she didn't want it neither. Fact of the matter was, I couldn't hardly eat a bite, I was in such a passion of hatred for that old man.

"What is the matter with you two young'uns?" Ma asked me and Sal, studying our faces. "Don't tell me you ain't hungry."

"I ain't feeling so good, Ma. Can I go and sit in Granny's room with her?" Sal said.

Ma frowned. "Well, I reckon so. Go on."

Sal got up and give old man Hooker a hateful glance and hurried out of the kitchen.

"And what is the matter with you, Arnold?" Ma asked.

"I ain't hungry neither," I answered, staring down at my plate.

Just then old man Hooker reached out and took that one-left roastin'ear from the platter and crunched into it with his gums. I'd of done anything if I could of slapped it right out of his dirty old hands!

"Well, go on then. You can feed Buck and Bill soon as we're through eating," Ma told me.

"If they is anything left!" I grumbled under my breath as I pushed my chair under the table.

"You're too easy on them young'uns!" I heard old man Hooker say out of his filled-up-with-food mouth as I walked away.

27

Ma had put a blanket over the storage room door so Granny could have some privacy and she put a feather mattress down for her to sleep on and a dresser someone give her for birthing a baby. Granny brought along a few family pictures and hung them on the walls and she set her brush and comb and other doodads on the shelves where Ma kept extry blankets and canned goods. When I passed through the blanket, Granny was setting in her rocking chair she'd brought with her, and Sal was setting down on the feather mattress on the floor. The room was small and cozy, but I knowed it wasn't the kind of room no one would want to live in.

"Arnold, you growed a whole one inch since you was in here yesterday!" Granny said as she looked up at me.

"Aw, no I ain't, Granny. You're just saying that," I told her with a blush.

"Now, bless me, you have too!" Granny insisted. "Ain't he growed a whole inch, Sally?" Granny looked down at Sal and Sal sort of smiled at me like she knowed I hadn't.

"Sure he has," Sal grinned. "Arney will soon be as big as Pa was."

We had got to where we could mention Pa without wanting to cry and I felt right proud to be compared with him. He had been big and tall with wide shoulders and strong legs, and I expected to be just like him.

I went over to Sal and sat down on the feather mattress with her. "How come you ain't eating, Granny?" I asked her.

Sal give me a secret punch in my arm with her elbow and whispered, "You know why!"

Granny pursed her lips up tight and narrowed her eyes at the wall across from her. "I'd ruther starve to death and have the vultures eat my bones than to set at the same table with the likes of Tice Hooker!" she said with a toss of her gray-haired head.

"No one can blame you for that, Granny," I told her.

"Tice Hooker ought to be taken to task!" Granny continued, with anger making her nose twitch and her wide-set blue eyes flash.

"Don't worry yourself about him, Granny," I said. "You can't never tell what might happen to a man as no good as he is."

Granny stopped rocking and leaned forward. "Won't nothing happen to him! Ought to though! It ought to! The way he treats folks is a sin and a shame! And it ain't just me I'm referring to. Look at the way he done poor Amelia, his own flesh and blood. Makes my old blood go to boiling just to think about it."

"Maybe something *will* happen," I repeated, and I looked down at my hands that was laying in my lap. Something was beginning to stir around in my brain.

"Like what?" Sal asked, and I could feel her eyes studying me.

"You can't never tell," I said, trying to make my words sound casual.

Sal stared at me until I had to look up at her. "What do you mean by that, Arney?" she asked, and her eyes was narrowed over me with a big curious look in them.

"How do I know? Can't a feller just talk?" I said real quick.

29

"Ma shouldn't of asked Tice Hooker to take supper with us," Sal said, giving her attention to Granny.

"Your ma done what she thought was right, Sally," Granny said in a softer voice. She had leaned back in her chair and went to rocking again. "Your ma's a good woman and follers the teachings of the Bible."

"Ain't nothing in the Bible says you got to invite the devil hisself right into your own home!" I blasted out.

"It says, 'Do unto others . . .'" Sal started, and I give her a look that cut her off fast.

Granny sighed. "It's plumb hard on a woman alone. I been alone so long I ought to know."

"How long you been alone, Granny?" Sal asked, and Granny sighed again and took off her glasses and rubbed her eyes. When she put them back on, she started in to telling how she'd lived below Brushy Mountain ever since her husband died and how the only place she had ever found peace was in her little house. "Ain't nothing sweeter and more calming than to look up on that mountain and see the lupins and poppies swaying in the wind when spring comes. I could see the whole mountain just about from my little kitchen winder . . ." When Granny mentioned her kitchen winder, her face went sad. That winder was in the house she rented from old man Hooker. The house he throwed her out of.

I got up and started to the blanket over the door. I didn't want to hear no more.

"Where are you going, Arnold?" Granny asked.

"I got to get ready to feed Buck and Bill," I told her, and I went through the blanket past the table in the kitchen and out the back door. I could see old man Hooker out of

30

the edge of my eyes as I went, still at the table eating like he would never fill up his old gut. Ma was at the stove dishing up the last of the gravy out of the iron skillet for him.

Outside it was getting dark. The moon was coming up over the fields and casting shadders everywhere. In the yard Buck and Bill looked up at me like they was asking me what I had in mind of doing. I went over and sat down on the ground with them and rubbed my hands along their long skinny backs, thinking hard. It just weren't fair ner right for old man Hooker to go on treating folks the way he done Amelia, Sal, and Granny. I didn't like the way he took advantage of Ma's goodness neither.

As I sat there scratching my hand along old Buck and Bill's backs, I commenced to get that same stirring in my brain that I'd felt when I was with Sal and Granny. All at once a feeling come over me that was so overpowering, it seemed to take me up in it like a whirlwind. A whirlwind that kept growing and growing, getting bigger and bigger until I felt I was being lifted plumb up off the ground by it. It was in that moment that I made up my mind. I was going to kill old man Hooker.

I heard the front door slam closed and I jumped up. I knowed that it would be old man Hooker leaving, starting on his way home. I left Buck and Bill and hurried around the side of the house and peered into the front yard. Old man Hooker was just going out the gate and heading down the road.

Without no more thinking, I knew what I had to do. I started to take off in a run after him, but suddenly Ma's voice split the air.

31

"Arnold! Come and get these scraps for the hounds!" she called from the back door.

"*What* scraps?" I grumbled as I watched old man Hooker disappear into the darkness. I turned around disgustedly and headed up to the house. Well, I'd get my chance again, and right soon, I hoped.

Chapter
5

I had my eyes on old man Hooker the next Sunday in church. He was wearing shoes then and a dark suit of clothes and he kept his head down low like he was afraid for the preacher to see all the meanness he had in him. Even when Preacher Jessup was shouting out loud enough to wake up all the dead-and-buried Indians up on Brushy Mountain, old man Hooker didn't raise his head. I knowed he couldn't be asleep. No one could sleep through Preacher Jessup's sermons.

I glanced across the aisle at Travis and Gussie setting together in their store-bought suits. They was both giving me and Sal a sneer. I hadn't reckoned with them yet over the last fight they'd had with Sal. Even though she got the best of them, they needed to be put in their places. I raised my hand and give them a doubled fist and narrowed my eyes at them. They looked away fast. That give me some satisfaction to know they was afraid of me. But I wasn't thinking about them too much. It was old man Hooker I had in my mind.

I knowed that just about every Sunday, whether he come

to church or not, he took a hike up into the foothills. Old as he was, he could climb like a snake slithering through heavy brush, over rocks and along narrow trails. He could outdo many a younger man.

When Preacher Jessup's sermon was over, everyone stood up to sing the last hymn. It looked like old man Hooker couldn't wait to get out of the church. I watched him twitching and moving around like he was ready to take off like a shot soon as everyone stopped singing. And that's exactly what he done. He whipped around, ignoring Mr. Satterfield's handshake, and beat it out the door, lickety-splittin' it across the yard before anyone else could even make it down the church steps. I hurried down the aisle, bumping into this one and that one, trying to stay close at his heels. By the time I got to the door, I seen him beating it across the churchyard with his head down and his hands clasped tightly behind him, walking so fast I knowed I'd have to run to keep up with him. It was my first chance to get him alone and I didn't want to miss it.

I was on the last step leading down from the church when someone reached out and grabbed my arm. I jerked around and looked right into Daphne Hazelton's wide, fat face.

"Where you going in such a rush, Arney? I ain't hardly seen you one whole minute except in school and even then you act like you'd ruther study books than talk to me. Looks like you'd want to slow down long enough to get an invite to my twelfth birthday party."

I glared at Daphne and pulled my arm away from her. It was just like her to come between me and what I wanted to do! She smiled at me and her big fat cheeks raised up on each side of her face like little hills. Daphne had huge yeller-green eyes like a cat and dishwater colored hair that hung like a limp rag all around her shoulders. She wasn't much to look at, but her ma sure could bake. Everyone went to Daphne's parties just so they could eat her ma's fine baked goods.

"What kind of cake you having?" I asked, practically licking my chops over the memory of that big chocolate walnut cake with two inches of dark, fudgy chocolate icing Daphne's ma had baked for her last birthday party.

"You know my mama." Daphne smiled even bigger and her cheeks rose higher. "She's bound and determined to outdo herself every year and bake the best cake in the whole county."

"You reckon it'll be chocolate?" I asked, with old man Hooker slipping out of my mind for the moment.

"Mama made chocolate last year," Daphne said, with her cheeks going down.

"Well . . ." I started scratching my chin. "I don't know. Chocolate has always been my most favorite . . ."

"Oh, Mama would bake a chocolate cake if I asked her to, Arney. I just know she would," Daphne said real fast.

"I'll be there," I told her, and I started walking across the yard. Daphne took off with me.

"What are you going to bring me for a present, Arney?" she asked eagerly, like she couldn't wait.

"Well, I don't rightly know. But you'll like whatever it is," I told her. Fact of the matter was, Ma picked out all of Daphne's birthday presents and I never knowed what they was until the last minute.

"Give me a hint, Arney. Will it be a necklace? Or a pretty ring?"

"I got to go," I said, and I took off in a run away from

her. If I'd let her, she would of stayed there all day pestering me about her birthday present.

But old man Hooker was back in my mind again and I had to beat a quick path out of the churchyard to try and catch up with him. I ran as hard and as fast as I could, until I spied him stomping along the road that led into the foothills. But, instead of heading up into the hills, he started walking along the cow path that runs next to the creek. I slowed down and snuck behind a tree to watch the old fool as he climbed up on the dirt bank overlooking the creek and stared down into the water. He just stood there for the longest time, looking into the water like his thoughts was far away. I watched him, my eyes narrowed over his skinny, hunched-over body, his head bent down, and his hands still clasped behind his back. No need to wait for him to go into the hills, I thought savagely. I can put him out of his misery right now!

I moved as quietly as I could to another tree that was closer to the bank of the creek and peered around the wide trunk. He was still standing there. Just watching the water like him and his thoughts was the only two things in the world. It was going to be easy just to sneak over and give him one good, hard, fast push right down into that water!

But as I started to move away from the tree, the old man suddenly let out a loud, wild yelp and went skiffing and slipping down the bank, sliding all the way into the water below! There was a hard, loud splash as he hit. I dashed out away from the tree and ran to a clump of bushes, eager to see how the old fool landed, hoping he'd hit headfirst! I yanked the leaves of the bushes apart and peered through them with my heart making a clattering sound in my ears like a train running over railroad tracks. The minute I seen him there with his arms flying around and his feet sloshing up and down in the water, struggling to get his balance, I felt my whole self fill up with pure joy! Now the old devil would get what was coming to him! Now he'd leave folks alone! Now everyone would be happy!

The water was swirling and splashing all around him as he tried to grab on to an old piece of branch from a tree that kept floating close, then would suddenly sail away from him. Good enough for you, you mean old thing, I wanted to shout. But all at once, he exploded with a loud, cracking cough that sounded like a plea for help and his last breath at the same time. His head went sinking down below the water and his feet and arms disappeared. I come out of the bushes and went to stand on the bank and peered down to get a better look. The water was still except for the bubbles and circles that waved and shuddered all around where the old man had gone down.

Fear come at me, snorting and charging like a bull. I felt like every hair on my head was standing straight up and the breakfast Ma had made me turned sour and threatened to come flying up out of me. There ain't no fear like that kind of fear. No sir.

I was off in a run before I even knowed my legs was moving, tumbling down through the sandy bank and making a splash in the water just as old man Hooker's head come up out of the bubbles and waves. He coughed and sputtered in a strangled way and his head disappeared again. My hands plunged down into the water, feeling full of strength and power, like they didn't even belong to me. They grabbed on to old man Hooker and pulled him to a flat place on the bank. He was so frail and thin, he didn't even feel no heavier than one of Ma's feather pillers. I laid him on his side and beat on his back until I could see water flowing out of his mouth and until he commenced to jerk and cough and explode with cuss words.

Soon as I heard them cuss words, I knowed the old devil was all right.

"Durn your old rotten hide, anyway!" I muttered under my breath as I felt the passion of hatred rise in me all over again. What had I done to save his old ungrateful skunk skin?

He coughed some more, hunched over, threw hisself into a sitting position and coughed again. I leaned down and beat on his back hard as I could and grumbled, "Well, looks like you'll live, dang it all!"

"Leave me be!" the old fool shouted, slinging out his arm at me and looking up at me with his eyes all red and watery.

I stood back, sighed me a deep, disgusted sigh and shook my head as I looked down at him. He shouted again, and I whipped around and beat it up the bank and away from the creek as fast as I could go, complaining to every tree that got in my way and to every old weed that I stomped down with my feet and to every bird that made a noise over my head, "I should of let that old fool drown! The dad-blasted old devil! I wish I'd never pulled him out of that creek!

I tramped back to the cow path in my wet clothes that Ma was sure to question me about, knowing that if I had it to do over again, I'd let Tice Hooker die for sure.

When I got home and went into the yard, Ma was there

sprinkling feed out to the chickens. They was all follering around her, clucking and cackling hungrily. Even Gobble was flying around, trying to get some of the feed.

Ma looked around, seen me and her mouth fell open. "What happened to you, Arnold?"

"Well, I . . . well, I fell into the creek."

"And in your best Sunday clothes too!" Ma said, shaking her head. "You had no business going around that creek in them clothes. You should of come home with me and Sally and Granny."

I went up on the porch and opened the door. "You sure are right about that, Ma," I said over my shoulder as I went through the door.

Chapter
6

When it come time for Daphne Hazelton's birthday party, I'd of ruther gone skunk hunting! But Ma made sure me and Sal both got dressed in the best clothes we had and that we took Daphne the paper tablet and pencil box she had picked up for presents at the Cash-and-Carry store. Sal put up a fuss about the dress she had to wear, but I thought it looked right nice. It had little blue flowers on it and made her gray-blue eyes look all blue. Ma had sewed on a pretty collar and belt. She had cut the material out of an old dress of hers.

Ma drove me and Sal to Daphne's house in the Ford, making sure we'd not wander off someplace else if we was left to walk. When she pulled up in front of the Hazeltons' place, there was already about ten kids out on the front porch all dressed up and tossing colored balloons back and forth. Music was coming from the Victrola inside the house, and there was several cars parked along the side of the house. Looked like there was lots of folks there to help celebrate Daphne's twelfth birthday.

"Now, you two be on your best behavior and, Arnold, don't you go to acting snippy with Daphne," Ma said as she stopped the car. "You know how important Daphne's birthday parties is to her."

"Only important thing to Daphne is Daphne," Sal muttered from the back seat. I was in the front seat with Ma.

"Now, Sally, you behave yourself," Ma spoke up.

Just as Ma said that, Daphne come flying off the porch and across the yard to the car. She was wearing a new-looking dress, one that Ma must of made for her, and her hair was all flopped out around her shoulders with a red ribbon stuck right on top of her head. Her eyes was all lit up and there was a big smile on her mouth that pushed her pudgy cheeks up and out. I glanced back at Sal. She was looking down at her dress. I wanted to tell her that she looked as good as Daphne Hazelton did any day, but Daphne reached the car before I could.

"Hi, y'all," Daphne said through the winder of the car and her wide smile got even wider. "I sure am glad to see you. Come on up to the house." She reached out and opened my door so I had to get out, much as I hated to. She didn't open the back door for Sal. And when Sal got out of the car, Daphne give her a critical up-and-down look. "Hello, Sally," she said like she would of preferred to ignore her. But she had a bead on the two presents Sal had in her hands, like she wondered why they was so small.

"Hello, Daphne," Sal said back, and I could tell she was plumb self-conscious about her dress and about how pretty Daphne's dress was.

I shut the car door and Daphne turned to look through the car winder at Ma. "Hello there, Miz Burdette," she said.

"Happy birthday, dear," Ma said. Then to me and Sal

she said, "I'll be back in two or three hours to get you."
She drove away and I wished I was going with her.

"I'll take those," Daphne said suddenly, and she reached
out and took the two presents out of Sal's hands. She lifted
each one and give it a good shake up close to her ear. Me
and Sal exchanged a look. When Daphne finished shaking
the presents, she looked back at me like she was disappointed they wasn't no big rattle to them.

I looked up on the porch at all them kids and I started
feeling like Sal felt in her made-over dress. Seemed like all
the boys was better dressed than me. They looked like they
was all shiny and spit-polished while I looked a little tar-
nished around the edges. I was wearing my best plaid shirt
and dark pants and my hair was combed back with plenty
of oil. I reckoned I must not of looked too bad, though, the
way Daphne glommed on to me. She fell into step right
beside me, leaving Sal to walk behind us alone. I glanced
back at her and she was walking with her head a little bit
down.

"Arney, do you know what I wish I'd get on my birthday?" Daphne asked, giving me another smile and not
waiting for me to answer. "I wish I'd get something extry
special from an extry special boy. It's not something you'd
get in a box neither. Can you guess what it is and *who* that
extry special boy is?" Them cheeks went back up like two
balloons getting ready to pop.

I could feel all that oil in my hair commence to drizzle
down the back of my neck and my palms to break out in a
sweat. I knowed who she meant, all right, and *what* she
meant!

"Well?" Daphne said, and she reached out and took
hold of my arm.

I cleared my throat. "I don't reckon I can," I told her.

"Just wait till I blow out the candles on my birthday cake," Daphne said in a little whisper up close to my face.

I yanked my arm away then and hurried up the steps of the porch. Sal ran up right behind me and disappeared into the balloons the kids was still tossing around. I hurried to get lost in them balloons too. I didn't reckon I wanted Daphne Hazelton hanging on to my arm and whispering close to my face, even if it was her birthday party and her ma had outdone herself on the cake.

Everyone was shouting and laughing, batting at them balloons and jumping all around and, the next thing I knowed, one hit me right in my face and a girl's laughter come tinkling through the noise, sounding like little bells. I looked around and seen Inez Porter setting on the porch railing, holding her hands over her mouth as she giggled.

Inez couldn't be called anything but pretty as she sat there in a pink print dress with her blond hair drawn back from her face and laying in waves along her shoulders. She was the only girl I ever seen with light hair and dark eyes. Her eyes was deep, smooth brown with no other color added and her skin was as clear and pale as fresh milk poured from a big pail. She was friendly and quiet and not always after you the way some girls was. For instance, Daphne Hazelton!

I smiled and went over to the railing and sat down beside Inez. The sweet smell of talcum powder rushed up into my face soon as I sat down.

"I'm sorry, Arney," Inez said, and she giggled a little when she said it.

"Aw, I ain't worried about no old balloon. They don't hurt like a baseball would."

43

"I was trying to hit Travis on his shoulder, but he jumped away just as you got close," she explained.

"Don't matter," I said.

"Well, I sure wouldn't throw an old hard baseball at you," Inez went on, and we both laughed, and suddenly I felt a funny feeling laughing with the prettiest girl on that porch and her talcum powder swirling all around me. I was glad when Daphne started calling out for everyone to settle down.

"Let's play Huckle Buckle Beanstalk," she said, and some of the kids protested and some of the others agreed to it. "You be first, Gussie. Go into the front room of the house and hide this jax ball . . ."

Gussie pushed his long dark hair out of his face, grabbed the ball out of Daphne's hand, and beat it through the door of the house.

"What you want to bet he hides it inside your ma's sewing basket?" Travis called out, laughing. Travis had light brown hair and red and brown freckles all over his face and arms, and blue eyes that lit up and danced when he laughed.

"Of course he will! That's why I chose him to go first, he's so dumb. I wanted to get *him* over with," Daphne said.

Everyone laughed and soon Gussie come swaggering out the front door with a big grin on his face. His long, stringy hair was all flopped in his eyes, as usual. Sometimes you couldn't even see his eyes for his rag-mop hair.

"You got it hid good, Gussie?" Daphne asked, and she turned and give everyone a wink.

"You'll never find it. Leastways not for a long, long time," Gussie answered with a big grin.

We all trooped into Daphne's front room and started searching for the jax ball. We looked high and low, in Miz Hazelton's sewing basket, under her pianer lid, behind cushions on the divan, even in Mr. Hazelton's cigar box. But that jax ball couldn't be found. Daphne was getting fuming mad over it too. She stood off with her hands on her hips glaring at Gussie. "Where'd you hide my jax ball, Gussie Bilbow?"

"Ain't fair to tell!" Gussie said with a hard frown on his face.

"That's right," everyone agreed.

Just then we all heard Miz Hazelton call out, "You young'uns go back out on the porch now. In just a little while we'll have our cake and ice cream."

We trooped back out on the porch and Daphne sat down in the glider swing and went to pushing back and forth in it hard. "You better tell me where my jax ball is, you little worm," she said with her eyes glued onto Gussie.

"He ain't supposed to tell," Travis spoke up.

"Telling ain't part of the game," someone else said, and we all agreed to that.

"It's *my* party and I can make up the rules if I want to!" Daphne snapped with her eyes flashing.

"You ain't a bit fair!" Sal said suddenly, and everyone turned to stare at her. "All you care about is your old ball and birthday presents and your old selfish self!"

My heart commenced to thump. I bit into my lip and held on to it. I could see all of Sal's resentment toward Daphne in her face. It wasn't the jax ball and it wasn't the presents and it *wasn't exactly* that Sal was jealous of Daphne. Sal sure was lots prettier. It was mostly Daphne's clothes and the way she was always sneering at the way Sal

45

dressed and the fact that Ma, being a seamstress along with everything else, sewed lots of Daphne's dresses, that's what burned at Sal.

Daphne stopped still in the glider swing and looked at Sal like she couldn't believe what she'd heard. "Why, Sally Burdette, you *know* that ain't a bit true," she said in a voice that suddenly turned so sweet it had the smell of sugary syrup dripping all around that porch. "I ain't like that at all. And, just to prove it, I want you to sing one of your made-up songs for everyone."

Sal mashed her mouth down hard and glared at Daphne. But everyone else commenced to beg her to sing. "Do it, Sal," I urged her on. There wasn't no one could make up songs the way Sal could ner sing them as sweet as she could neither.

"Oh, please, Sally," Inez begged. Sal looked at her and her mouth softened. "Sing us the song about the way the lupins and poppies look in the hills in spring."

"Please, Sal," Daphne said.

"Well, all right," Sal finally said. "But I'll just sing a little bit and that's all."

Sal got up and stood in the center of the porch and folded her hands together in front of her. She looked down at her hands for a minute and I knowed she was trying to think up the words about the lupins and poppies. We all sat or stood around giving her our full attention. After a little, she cleared her throat, took in a deep breath and commenced to sing. The words was quick and perky, and she kept time to them, tapping her left foot against the wood floor. A little breeze blew in from both sides of the porch and wiggled the curls in her hair. It was a pure pleasure to hear Sal sing. Even Miz Hazelton and some of the ladies in the house with her come to the door to listen. Inez's mother, Miz Porter, was with them.

> *"Spring is here . . . it is clearrrrr . . .*
> *When everywhere I look . . . everything I seeeee . . .*
> *Is . . .*
> *Loopity-Loo Lupins . . .*
> *Poppity-Pop Poppies . . ."*

When Sal was done singing her song everyone clapped their hands and Miz Hazelton said in the doorway to the other ladies, "Don't that child just beat all you ever seen?"

Everyone agreed to that and kept up asking Sal to sing another one of her made-up songs. While they was all making suggestions and calling out things like, "Make up one about Miz Tinker at school," and "Make up one about summer and school nearby being out." Miz Porter called out to Inez to come into the house and help her with something.

Inez got up and smiled at me. "I'll be back in a little," she said, and she walked away with her talcum powder smell follering her.

"When are we going to get that cake?" someone asked impatiently, and someone else batted some balloons up to the porch ceiling and everyone jumped up to have a chance at them. When the balloons floated back down, the kids commenced to yell and holler and push at each other, trying to get to them first. While this was going on, Daphne got up out of the glider swing and come over to me. She scooted back on the porch railing and sat down beside me, crossing her leg and fluffing out her skirt. I could feel her eyes on me, but I didn't want to look at her.

"Arney, I've decided I ain't going to wait any longer to

47

tell that extry special boy what it is I want more than any-thing for my birthday," Daphne said, and I swallered hard. Three whole times. But my throat still felt dry.

I turned to look at her finally. "Y-you ain't?" I croaked out of my dry throat.

"No, I ain't," she said, and her eyes was as big and round as her face was wide. She moved a little closer to me and I felt her fat arm touch mine.

I took in a deep breath and wished I could be tossing balloons! Next thing I knowed, Daphne's face was so close to mine I could feel my cheek grow damp from her breath.

"I want an extry special kiss for my birthday from that extry special boy right now, Arney," Daphne said, and I drew back and glared at her.

"I got to go!" I said, and I jumped up, whirled around and started plunging off as fast as I could, bumping into kids that was still jumping for them balloons and feeling several of them plunk me in the back and on my arms. Suddenly they was a loud POP noise and I trembled all over. I'd stepped on a balloon and it exploded under my foot!

"Where are you going, Arney?" I heard Daphne yell out as I reached the steps and flew down them. "Come back here, Arney! It's my birthday!"

I snuck a look around once and seen Daphne leaning over the porch rail on her squat arms. They was a look of hurt on her face and a frown that would of made my heart tender except that I wasn't going to hang around and make her birthday wish come true. Not even with the strong de-sire in me for her mama's chocolate walnut cake!

Chapter

7

I flew across Daphne's yard like I'd sprouted wings and headed off down the road with the music from the Victrola follering right at my heels. Down the road a ways, I seen Moonstruck Mulligan walking toward me. Old Moonstruck used to preach at the church until he commenced to act strange. He took to sleeping out under the stars every night and to going up and down the road playing on his juice harp and preaching to anyone who would listen. Granny Stallcup claimed Moonstruck got electrified by the rays of the moon from sleeping under it too much and that's how he come to be the way he was. That's how he got his name too. When he got too bad, folks voted him out of the church and voted Preacher Jessup in.

You could see Moonstruck on the road any time, day or night. But you could never tell he slept out in the open. He had his clothes done up by Lessie Fay at the Boarding House. He always wore bright flannel shirts and a wide-brimmed straw hat to keep the sun off his head, and his overalls was creased so sharp by Lessie Fay's flat iron that they looked like they was slit all the way down to his big, wide brogans. Looked to me like a feller that took such good care of hisself had to be smarter than folks give him credit for. He carried his juice harp in the bib pocket of his overalls, and it never took much for him to snap it out and go to playing on it. Most likely he'd cut into a fast jig right there in the road too. Sometimes he et at Lessie Fay's Boarding House, but most usually he had a gunnysack tossed over his shoulder with turnips or wild berries in it to eat.

"Goodday to you, Arnold Burdette," Moonstruck said to me when he got close and he tipped his straw hat.

"Where you headed?" I asked him, and he stopped and set his gunnysack down on the tops of his brogans and smiled.

"I'm on my way to glory, boy. And this here is the glory road we're traveling on. It's paved with gold and it'll hurt your eyes if you look at it too long."

I ran my hand across my face to cover my grin and said, "Moonstruck, looks to me like, the way you talk, you'd want to go back to the church."

"See that rock over yonder, boy?" He stuck out his arm stiff and straight and pointed to the side of the road where a rock, big enough to lay down on, sat. "That's my church. I can set on it and look out over that field of wild flowers and go to church right here in my heart." He jabbed at his chest with his thumb.

I glanced out over the field where a hundred different wild flowers swayed together in the breeze, mixing their colors all up. Then I looked back at Moonstruck. "What you got in that gunnysack?" I asked.

50

"I got the wine of good and the wine of evil in it. I got it in bottles too strong to break. Even a big feller like your daddy was couldn't break these here bottles."

I stared at the gunnysack laying limp across Moonstruck's brogans. It looked like it might of had one or two turnips in it. There he goes again, talking like a fool, I thought and I turned my head and chuckled, even though I tried not to. "Where you taking that wine?" I asked when I could get my head turned back around.

"I'm taking it to the taking place, to the making place, to the place of eternal light."

I snickered and coughed over it to try and cover it. "Where is that, Moonstruck?"

"Why, the place where good is separated from evil, that's where, boy," he answered like he thought I ought to know. Then he picked up the gunnysack, tossed it over his shoulder, took out his juice harp, stuck it in his mouth and went to playing it.

I stood there watching him as he went off down the road skipping and jumping from one side to the other, keeping time to the music he played on his juice harp. Finally I turned around and started walking on my way.

As I walked, I started thinking about Moonstruck's wine of good and wine of evil. It sure was a mystery to me, but in a way I reckoned there might just be such a wine. Seemed like, if a feller wanted to be good, he'd take a sip of the wine of good. But if he wanted to be bad, he'd take a sip of the evil wine. It didn't make much sense that anyone would want to sip evil wine when they could taste the good wine, though.

All of a sudden old man Hooker's face come before me

51

on the road. It was right there in the gritty soil! The ruts was his deep wrinkles, his eyes was little beady-looking pebbles, his mouth was a small, narrow stick, and his ears was lumpy clods of dirt. I shivered just to look at that mean old face. "The wine of good and the wine of evil," I snorted. Well, it was sure, if anyone ever was evil, it was that no-good, meaner-than-the-devil-hisself, Tice Hooker! I took off in a run, slamming my feet right across the old face in the dirt and didn't stop running until I reached the house.

Granny was setting on the front porch rocking in Ma's old high-backed rocking chair with her mouth all pursed up and her eyes looking far off across the yard. She didn't even notice me come up until I set down on the step.

"What are you doing home, Arnold? Ain't you supposed to be at the Hazelton girl's party?" Granny asked.

"Yes, ma'am," I answered, leaning back against the porch post.

"Well, why ain't you there?"

"Aw . . . well . . ." I started, and I stopped and turned to watch Buck and Bill as they come sidling around from the corner of the house. When they seen me they come bounding up on the step and laid down close to me. I reached out and started smoothing down their hair.

"You runned away, didn't you," Granny said.

"I reckon I did," I admitted.

"I thought you liked going to parties."

"Sometimes," I said as Gobble come strutting by and went to poking around in the flower bed where Ma's morning glories and sweet peas was planted next to the fence.

52

Granny sighed a big, deep sigh and I turned and looked back at her. She was running the bottom of her apron over her eyes. "What's wrong, Granny?" I asked her.

"Seems like I'm under the force of despair. Have been ever since I was made to leave my little house." She laid the apron down in her lap and went to fiddling with the corner of it. "I had me some sweet peas and sweet williams and morning glories and a nice little shade tree to sit out under all summer long. I had me my own broom to sweep my floors with and my own stove to cook on and . . . as grateful as I am to your mother for taking me in, it just ain't the same. Lord knows, it just ain't the same as having my own little place," Granny said and sniffled and raised the corner of her apron to wipe over her eyes again.

I looked back at Gobble just as he raised his wings and flew across the yard to the pyrocantha bushes and started nibbling on the leaves. All the time my eyes was on him, I wasn't really watching him at all. I was seeing Tice Hooker's face like I'd seen it in the road and hating him all the more. It commenced to gnaw away at me like one of them ornery ticks that sometimes burrows down deep into Buck and Bill's hide. Once in a while one digs down so deep we have to burn it out. That's the feeling I had. Like I could feel one of them ticks burrowing down deeper and deeper in my skin and, no matter what I tried to do to get it out, I never could. I clean hated that old man for what he'd done to Granny.

"Yes, I'm under the force of despair," Granny said again in a sad voice. But after a little while she started in to singing a hymn and I reckon it made her feel better.

Later that day, after Ma brought Sal home from

Daphne's party and got finished fussing at me for leaving, Sal come up to me in my room and said, "Know where Gussie hid that old jax ball of Daphne's, Arney?"

"Where?" I asked her, stretching out on my bed and putting my hands behind my head.

"Right smack dab in the middle of Daphne's birthday cake! He punched it down and smoothed the frosting over it and no one knowed until Miz Hazelton went to cut into it. She near about had a hissy and Daphne was so mad, she chased Gussie out of the house and all the way out of the yard and told him he could never come to one of her parties again."

I commenced to laugh like I'd never stop. "Well," I said when I finally settled down, "looks like I wasn't the only one to miss out on Daphne's fine birthday cake."

Chapter
8

Summer vacation was still a week off but I managed to avoid Daphne just fine until a few mornings later. Sal and me was on our way to school bright and early and was crossing over the field where the weeds was flattened out to make a path to walk on when Daphne come running up behind us, calling out. Me and Sal looked back. Daphne was getting closer, swinging her lunch sack, her limp hair flying all over her face. Behind her Travis and Gussie walked with their heads together.

When Daphne reached us, me and Sal give each other a look, and Sal slowed down her walking and let Daphne walk next to me. I looked back to give Sal a disgusted glance, but she was looking at Daphne's pretty yeller dress and didn't even notice.

"Where you been, Arney? I been looking for you everywhere."

I shot a quick, half-guilty look at her. "I seen you lots of times," I told her.

"*Seen* me, yes. But being *with* me is two different things. Ever since you runned away from my birthday party, you been treating me like I had fleas or something."

"No, I ain't," I said.

"Yes, you have. And my mama even baked that chocolate walnut cake just for you. She said she'd never bake another one that I begged her to bake because of some boy."

"I didn't ask you to beg your mama to bake that cake," I said.

"Well, you more or less did!" Daphne said with a sullen look at me. "I was too embarrassed to even think of a thing to say after you took off the way you done. Seemed to me like you was afraid or something."

"I ain't afraid of nothing!" I said, but Daphne just went right on talking.

"You're the only boy I ever heard of that is afraid to kiss a girl! Why, there ain't nothing to kissing a girl. All's you got to do is pucker up your lips and set them on top of the girl's lips and press down a little. Ain't you never seen no one kiss before?"

I could feel my face getting hot and red and my insides getting ready to explode. But before I could do that, Sal jumped in between me and Daphne and repeated what I'd said. "My brother ain't afraid of nothing!"

Daphne turned her face to Sal and narrowed her eyes. "He is too! He's afraid to kiss a girl!"

Sal stopped, shoved her chin out, put her hands on her hips and shouted, "He is not! My brother is brave enough to kiss any girl! Even *you*, Daphne Hazelton!"

I swallered hard and glared at Sal. Her voice had raised and bellered out over the field. From behind us I could hear Travis and Gussie laughing. I jerked my head around to yell at them, and suddenly they was right there, caught up to us and looking at me with big grins on their faces.

"If you ain't afraid, why don't you prove how brave you are?" Travis asked me with a smirk on his face in place of that grin. The bright sun made his red and brown freckles pop out even more and in some places they seemed to run together like smears of paint.

I stared at him, swallering over and over, and feeling my ears turn hot. Travis and Gussie stood next to Daphne now. Sal was next to me. I give her a look that told her I wished she'd kept her mouth shut about how brave I was. Gussie started snickering like he couldn't stop and his dark, stringy hair flopped over onto his face and into his eyes just like it always done. I still hadn't reckoned with them two for fighting with Sal.

"He's afraid to prove it because it ain't true!" Daphne said, adding her own sneer at me.

"I . . . ain't neither!" I shouted.

"You are too!" Travis said, and he curled his lips at me.

I was all set and ready to bring up how him and Gussie was always onto Sal when Sal popped up and said to Travis, "I'd like to see *you* kiss a girl! I bet you'd run and hide if you was asked to!"

Travis's freckles flashed red, he looked so embarrassed. "I . . . I wouldn't neither," he said feebly.

"Oh, *yes* you would!" I said evenly, glad that Sal had got the best of him. That was reckoning enough for me. For *that* time, anyways.

Gussie turned to Travis. "Yeah, why don't *you* prove it?" he said.

"Huh?" Travis grunted, and his eyes got as big as them little eyes could ever get and he stared at his best friend like he couldn't believe Gussie was actually challenging him.

"I know what!" Daphne said with her eyes lit up and

her cheeks raised high in a wide grin. "We could have a kissing game right here!"

I stamped my foot good and hard in the weeds. "We ain't going to have no kissing game!"

Daphne's cheeks went down and she stared at me. Travis and Gussie looked at each other. I could hear Sal breathing with relief close to me. Suddenly Daphne whipped around, poked her nose in the air and marched away from us. "If Inez Porter was here, I bet you'd kiss her!" she throwed across her shoulder. I could feel my eyes bug out, I was so startled to hear her say that. Then she stopped and turned around and shouted, "I ain't never going to invite none of y'all to my birthday parties ever again!" Then she whipped back around.

Seemed like we all breathed a heavy, relieved sigh at that. Me and Sal started walking, and Travis and Gussie fell behind us and no one said another word all the way to school.

Later that day, during recess time, Travis come up to me in the play yard and said, "Guess what? Me and Gussie found some sticks of dynamite down by the railroad tracks the other day."

"Dynamite? What was dynamite doing by the railroad tracks?" I asked, plumb dumbfounded.

"How should I know? It was just laying there. They was two sticks of it and it ain't been shot off neither."

"What are you going to do with it?" I asked.

"I don't know. Save it for the Fourth of July maybe. I got it hid in my barn so's my Pa won't find it."

"What if he does find it?"

"If he gets suspicious, I'll just hide it somewheres else,"

Travis answered, and he stuck his hands down in his pockets, give me a little smile and sauntered off.

Folks said Travis Satterfield's Pa could find a needle in a haystack. I reckoned old Travis ought to be mighty careful. But not just because of his Pa. I knowed dynamite was awful dangerous. It wasn't nothing like firecrackers. And it sure wasn't nothing to fool around with.

When school let out, Sal took off walking with some of her friends and I started into town to pick up some flower seeds for Ma at the Cash-and-Carry store. They was for Granny so she could plant a little flower bed all her own at the side of the house. I was going to pull weeds for her and get the ground fixed a little before she commenced to plant the seeds.

On the way back from the store, I could see something that looked like smoke swirling up from the tops of the trees. I raised my nose and sniffed at the air. It was smoke, all right. I stood for a minute staring up at it, trying to calculate just where it come from. As I watched, it seemed to biller out even more and to cover the eastern part of the sky with a dark meanness. I shoved the sack of seeds into my back pocket and took off in a run, follering the smell and the dark clouds.

I hurried through Miz Pine's back lot, down the road away from town, hotfooting it across Charley Parlier's field, running until I was plumb wore out, hoping all the while to get to that fire before someone was hurt in it. I was afraid it might be my own house on fire or Jeb Worth's barn with his horses in it. In my mind, I could see Ma and Granny in a wild dither, trying to get things out of the house and Jeb's fine horses rearing up against the flashing fire, kicking their heels at the stall doors, trying to get free. It made my heart pound with fear as I ran and ran. But when I got to Jeb's property, the horses was out in the pasture grazing and the barn wasn't on fire at all. Over the top of his barn I could see the sky above my place was blue and clear. Everything was peaceful and still like it always was.

Now the smoke appeared to be flying into the sky from the direction of the foothills. The foothills! Old man Hooker's place sat right at the bottom of them weedy hills with not another place around it. Could it be his place, I wondered? I kept running until I had almost reached the foot of Brushy Mountain where them weedy hills began. Then I slowed down, panting for my breath, and walked as slow as I could, on purpose. Pretty soon I come to a fence that ran along a piece of vacant property, stopped, and placed my arm up over the wood post and leaned against it. I raised my other arm and mopped the sweat off my face and watched a hawk circling the sky where the smoke was burning into the air. Birds commenced to call out all around me in the trees along the road. I turned my head, looking from tree to tree. Suddenly it seemed like all them birds was chittering and squawking and flitting around in a nervous fury, like they was trying to make me understand something important. But there wasn't no need for them to tell me anything. By then I knowed it was old man Hooker's place on fire!

Chapter
9

It was old man Hooker's place on fire, all right. And most likely he was in that shack all alone. What if he can't get out? I wondered. Then I stopped wondering real fast.

"What do I care? I ain't going to find out!" "You got to go!" "No, I ain't going!" "Arney, you got to go!" "No!" "Yes!" *Blame it all, anyway!*

My mind kept up a running battle all the time I stood there leaning against that fence post watching the smoke get blacker and blacker in the sky. I'd make up my mind not to go and see about the old coot and his durned fire and next thing I knowed, that voice inside me would be telling me to go.

"Ain't this what I wanted?" I shouted out once. "Ain't this what that *old fool* deserves?"

On top of this, them birds just kept up a hoop and a hurrah, swooping down and landing on the fence and staring bold as life, right into my eyes, as if *they* was telling me, "You'd better go, Arnold Burdette, or you'll be sorry for the rest of your life!"

"Sorry!" I blasted out at one of them durned nosy birds that wouldn't even blink its eyes and just only kept staring at me. "What would I be sorry for? Far as I'm concerned, that whole place of old man Hooker's can burn right on down to the ground and him along with it! Sorry? Not me! No sir!" I felt like a fool standing there blasting out at that little old bird, but it had no business setting on that fence trying to make me feel guilty.

I stomped my foot into the hard ground, swiped the sweat off my face again and, when I looked back up, I seen a huge black vulture perched on the next fence post, just a little ways down, staring at me like he was accusing me of something too horrible to even mention.

"Well? Well? What are you looking at me for?" I raised my voice up in a wild yell and he took off, spreading his huge wings wide, tilting through the air back and forth across the smoky sky, over the fields and road, looking down at me and hissing accusingly. Blobs of guilty sweat broke out all over me and my mouth went so dry, it felt like I'd et dust for breakfast.

Then, all at once, seemed like from every tree and bush along the road, from out of the fields and down from the sky, from behind the wildflowers and rocks and the fence, birds commenced to fly around crazily, making their strange sounds loud and louder and *even louder,* until the whole world appeared like it was alive with nothing but the earsplitting noises they made.

"CAW-CAW!" "KILLY-KILLY-KILLY!" "TSEER-TSEER-TSEER!" "WHIT-WHIT!" "TEE-TEE-TEE!" "CHEEP-CHEEP!" "YACUP-YACUP!" "KROOK-KROOK!" "KASHEEK-KASHEEK-KASHEEK!" "WHEW-WHEW-WHEW!"

62

The sounds mixed together like vegetables in Ma's beef stew, being stirred round and round until I had to slam my hands over my ears to shut it all out. But still the sound come, only now the strangeness of it turned into words. Words that sounded like, "ARNOLD BURDETTE, YOU GOT TO HELP TICE HOOKER! GO! GO! GO! TSEER . . . WHIT . . . TEE . . . KILLY . . . YACUP . . . KROOK . . . GO! WHEW! KASHEEK . . . CHEEP . . . CAW-CAW! *GO! RUN!*"

Finally, against my own will, even against all the hate that boiled inside me, I jerked away from the fence and my feet started walking under me, faster and faster, while them birds flew back and forth above my head.

"MYAK-MYAK! *RUN!* KASHEEK-KASHEEK! *RUN!* TSEER-TSEER! *RUN, ARNOLD, RUN!*"

My feet stumbled ahead of me, faster and faster, until I was running down the road, all of them birds flying around me, ahead of me, behind me, like they was an ocean of water surrounding me, and like the sounds they made was waves pushing me on and on toward the clouds of rolling smoke that filled the sky.

I kept running even faster, panting and breathless, and feeling like I'd fall flat on my face in the road. When I reached where I could see what was burning, I realized I was all alone, surrounded by stillness. I looked up and around. The birds and their terrible screeching and squawking noises was gone.

Chapter

10

Old man Hooker's shack sat on a large piece of open, rocky land with an old barn that was half-tumbled down, a dried-up well, and a lot of dry eucalyptus trees with huge, tangled branches. It was a hot, dry, ugly place that was always parched with dust except when there was a good rain. When the old man's well went dry, he took to carrying water from Jeb Worth's place. He never did try to dig deeper for water. Without water, the whole place was a menace to its own self. But, so far, there was only the two big eucalyptus trees that sat closest to the shack that was burning. The black smoke was roaring up from them and the fire was just beginning to lap at the shack.

I stood at the edge of the yard watching the shack, wondering if old man Hooker was in it. I coughed a little from the smoke, rubbed my eyes, squared off my legs and hitched my fingers through the belt loops on my pants and called out, "Hey, you mean old thing, you in there?" But I knowed, at that distance, he couldn't of heard me even if he was. All at once the roof of the shack caught fire from the trees. I brought my legs together quick and stood there stiff as a board, watching it ignite and shoot out red and orange and yeller flames. What if that old fool was in that shack asleep, and I just stood there watching it go up in smoke? All at once the sound of them birds come back to me in a frenzy and, before I knowed what I was doing, my legs was moving under me and I was headed right to the shack.

As I ran, a limb split away from one of the eucalyptus trees and fell with a loud, crashing noise onto the roof of the shack. The whole roof seemed to explode with fire that licked out in every direction with a red and yeller and black tongue. I started pounding on the door with a fury and yelling out, "You in there, Tice Hooker?" But the only sound I heard was the crackling of the fire as it et away at the old, dry wood of the roof.

I beat on the door again and again and yelled, "Open the door! Your place is on fire!" But there was no answer from old man Hooker.

Out to the side of my eye I could see small, fiery-colored twigs and leaves fall away from the eucalyptus trees and start crawling into the dry, straw-colored hills, lapping at the sun-baked weeds and wild flowers. I commenced to bang on the door again. It was so hot it singed my knuckles.

"If you're in there, you got to come out!" I shouted, and I shoved my shoulder up against the hot door, feeling the heat through my shirt. The door give way and I went crashing into the shack, stumbling and almost falling onto the floor. I stood for a second to get my balance and felt my lungs fill up with smoke. I commenced to cough and look all around. The roof was crackling and popping like a bonfire above my head and I could feel the heat like I was ready to be burned up.

"TICE HOOKER!" I yelled and coughed. "TICE HOOKER!"

There was a sound that wasn't the crackle of the fire, and I looked in the direction it come from. There he was, laying on a cot, half-covered up with an old blanket, looking like he was sound asleep or dead, maybe. I couldn't tell which. And I didn't have time to speculate on it. But, as I watched him laying there with what appeared like a look of contentment on his old face, a new hatred run through me for all he'd done to folks.

I started to turn and rush out of the shack, when a part of the roof fell into the room with that tree limb burning and hissing all through what was left of the place. I fought with a wild fury to turn and run out the door. I cussed myself with the fiercest cuss words I knowed. Mostly they was ones I'd heard from old man Hooker hisself! I tried to spin on my heels and escape from that burning shack, leaving that old coot to lay there and disintegrate into the flames that was beginning to surround him. But all of a sudden, before I even knowed what I was doing, I lunged through the smoke to the cot and started dragging and pulling, yanking and lifting the old man across the floor. Just as we got through the door I heard a loud crash that sounded like a part of the walls had caved in. I commenced dragging and pulling him again, all the way across the yard, through the dirt and rocks and weeds, until I got him near the road and could lean him up against one of the euc trees. I stumbled back away from him then and bent over, coughing and staggering around, trying to get clean air in my lungs. When I could stop coughing, I went up close to the old man and felt for his heart. I could hear it thump-thumping through his bony chest. He wasn't dead, but I could hear his breath coming slow and heavy, like he was struggling for it. I leaned down on one leg and give his back a good hard slap and shook his thin shoulders, trying to make him cough. He lurched forward, exploding with barking coughs, wheezing and choking, just like when I pulled him out of the creek. Soon as he could stop and he got his wind back, his eyes sprang open and he glared at me like I was some kind of wild animal that had tried to attack him. Then he threw his arm out and hit me with his folded fist. I jumped back, stumbled and went sprawling.

"Get away from me!" he shouted, gagging and rasping.

I jumped up, mad as an old bull. "Dad-blast your durned old hide, anyway!" I yelled at him with my fists doubled into knots. "I should of let you burn into a bacon crisp! I should of left you in your old shack to burn into hell where you belong!"

I hated that old man so much I wished I *was* a wild bull and could trample right over him! I kicked my brogans so hard into the ground that my toes hurt.

"Ungrateful old fool! Mangy old dog!" I muttered as I turned to walk down the road. But, by then, folks was appearing from all over in cars and trucks and hay wagons with big barrels and washtubs filled with water. They come flying into the yard one after the other, shouting and yelling at each other and jumping down from the trucks, forming a line to pass buckets of water to splash onto the old shack. But the shack was near about gone and not even

67

worth wasting water on. Looked like the only thing left on the place was the old barn that was full of bats and spiderwebs and rats. Everyone turned their attention to the eucalyptus trees and the fire on the hill. Men started rushing up into the small flames that burned at the weeds and commenced to slap heavy blankets over them. Women was running along behind them, tossing buckets of water over everything.

"If this fire gets ahead of us, it'll move toward the mountain!" someone on the hill called out.

Smoke was swirling all around and folks was coughing and putting wet handkerchiefs over their faces, but they kept right on beating at the flames. Someone finally called out, "It won't reach the mountain! We've got a bead on it!"

"How did it get started?" someone else finally shouted, and Charley Parlier, standing on the hill, pulled his handkerchief away from his face and pointed to the side of the shack where a half-burned pile of kindling wood and ashes sat on the ground and a black pot laid, turned over on its side.

"A spark must of flew up into the euc trees and took hold," someone else shouted out.

"Tice was warned time and again about cooking under them dry trees," Charley Parlier added and covered his face with his handkerchief again. Then he leaned over and went to whipping at the weeds with an old blanket.

As I stood there watching and listening and wishing I'd never seen Tice Hooker in all my life, much less saved his old fool life, Jeb Worth come bouncing into the yard in his flatbed truck and jumped out of it. He stood beside the truck for a second with his hands on his hips, looking the situation over, then shook his head and said disgustedly, "I told Tice to get that well dug deeper so's he'd have water in case of an emergency, but he was too bull-headed stubborn to do it!" He looked at me. "Is he all right?" he asked, and he looked to where the old man was leaning against the euc tree. Now they was women gathered all around him with cups of water trying to get him to take drinks, and leaning down, patting him on his shoulder.

"I reckon he'll live. He's too mean to die," I grumbled under my breath.

But Jeb heard me and threw back his head and laughed big and loud. "Why, son, I hear tell you saved the old man. You ought to be right proud of yourself. You got second thoughts now?" He patted my arm, grinning at me.

Jeb was tall with shoulders about as broad as Pa's was and legs so thick and muscled they looked as strong as steel. He had sandy-colored hair and a sandy-colored mustache and eyes that was full of hazel-colored twinkles. He'd been a close friend of Pa's and I reckon there was times he felt responsible to keep an eye out for all of us. I grinned back at him. We both knowed how cussed ornery old man Hooker was.

"Well," Jeb went on, "I reckon I'll go over there and see if the old man has anything to say for hisself." He walked away and I started to foller him when I heard someone call my name. I looked around.

"Folks is saying you pulled Tice Hooker out of his shack. Is it true, Arney?" It was Inez Porter, standing on her Pa's hay wagon, surrounded by other people who had come to help put the fire out. Her blond hair was braided up over the top of her head like a halo and her brown eyes was looking right into mine.

"I reckon," I answered. "I reckon I done that." I ran my hand across my face to swipe the tears out of my eyes that the smoke made and that's when I seen that my hands, both of them, was as black as tar. I wanted to stick them in my pockets and hide them from Inez. But I didn't.

"Are you hurt, Arney? Your clothes is all torn," Inez said with a concerned-looking frown.

I looked down the front of me and, sure enough, my shirt was all raggedy like it had been singed by the fire and I didn't even know it. I looked back up at Inez on the hay wagon. "I'm okay," I said.

Inez turned and started pulling on her mama's belt. Miz Porter was bent down, facing the other way, dipping a bucket down into a tub full of water. "Mama! Arney Burdette saved Tice Hooker's life!" she said excitedly.

Miz Porter turned around and looked down at me and a big smile come across her face. "Well, that makes you a hero, Arnold," she said.

I looked down at the ground. Some hero, I thought disgustedly. If Inez and her mama knowed what my true feelings was, they wouldn't be thinking of me as no hero!

"Give the boy some water, Inez," Miz Porter said, and I looked up just as Inez dipped a big tin cup into a bucket of water.

"T-that's all right," I said, starting to back away. "I ain't thirsty."

Inez leaned down with the cup anyway, and I reached up, starting to take it, but she moved it back a little. "Let me hold it for you. Your hands is so black, they could be hurt."

Inez held the cup to my lips and I swallered one big gulp of water after another, looking up into her eyes all the while. She was looking down into mine at the same time, and it was all I could do not to swaller my tongue along with the water!

When the cup was empty and Inez took it away from my lips she said, "See there? You was dry."

I swiped my hand across my wet mouth, forgetting that it would leave a trace of black on my lips. Inez laughed and stood up.

"Would you like a ride home, Arnold?" Miz Porter asked me.

"N-no, ma'am. I'll go on by myself," I told her.

After a quick glance up at Inez, I turned and started walking off. I didn't go right home. I cut over to the creek and washed my face and hands off in the water and laid down in the cool grass at the bottom of the bank where the water made a little lapping noise and the frogs croaked softly to each other. The smell of smoke was still in the air and the sound of folks working to get the fire out come across the fields and over the trees, sounding dreamlike and far away. I closed my eyes. Some "other" part of me must of, on secret, drank the wine of good that Moon-struck Mulligan told me about. Fact of the matter was, I must of got drunk off it to of saved that old ungrateful fool's life a *second* time!

The only thing that made me feel a bit good about what

71

I'd done was the hope that now the old devil would go away from Weedpatch and never come back. His daughter was gone and his shack was gone and his well was dry and there wasn't nothing I knowed of to keep him in town. He'd be doing me and everyone else a big favor by getting as far away as he could.

Chapter

11

I reckon I slept, laying there beside the creek, because the next thing I knowed, I opened my eyes and darkness was hovering over everything. I jumped up and looked around. The sun had gone down and heavy shadders fell across the water. The frogs had stopped croaking and the crickets had took over. Ma would sure be wondering what had happened to me and them seeds she'd sent me to buy. I reached around and checked my back pants pocket. Then I checked the other one. The seeds was gone. Wasn't nothing to do but go on home and tell Ma I'd lost them. I reckoned she'd be mighty upset with me when she found it out.

When I walked into the yard I stopped cold. Parked in front of the house was Vesper Gene De Goff's old rattle-bang pickup with the one headlight missing and the winder glass cracked on one side, and the Beckers' and Pines' cars and Preacher Jessup's car and Sage Johnson's Model T Ford and the Hazelton's black Plymouth. There wasn't hardly no room for the chickens to strut around in, they was so many cars there.

I started to walk again and went up to the porch and seen that Jeb Worth's flatbed truck was parked to the side of the house. I took me in a deep breath and went on up the porch steps. I reckon Ma no more than heard the first creak of the boards in the floor under my feet, than she was at the door and pushing the screen open.

"Ma," I said before she could say anything. "I lost the seeds you give me the money to buy."

A big smile broke out on Ma's face. "The news is all over the place about how you saved Tice Hooker's life, Arnold," she said, and she gathered me into her arms and squeezed me and kissed me on my cheeks and forehead. Then she pulled me through the door and there, right in the front room, was all the folks who owned them cars parked in the yard. Every chair in the house was being used and it looked like the seat of the divan was sunk down from the weight of all them folks setting on it. My eyes went around the room, taking it all in. I felt as awkward as an old plow mule being invited to a Sunday dinner. Everyone was staring at me with big smiles on their faces while the little kids ran back and forth across the room playing tag. I seen Daphne Hazelton setting on the pianer bench smiling at me and I looked away real quick.

"Look at you, boy! Ain't you something!" Granny Stallcup said, and I could feel Ma's hand on my shoulder.

"Your pa would be mighty proud, son," Preacher Jessup said from the center of the divan.

"Bravest feller in the whole county!" Jeb Worth said from a corner of the room where he was sipping at a cup of coffee. There was a smile on his face and that twinkle he gets in his eyes.

"Where'd you get all that spunk, Arney?" Vesper Gene asked. It looked like he had as much grease on his face as I had singed threads on my shirt!

"He gets it from his Daddy," Sage Johnson spoke up to answer Vesper Gene's question.

"Amen to that," Preacher Jessup said. "Morris was a fine and honorable man."

Folks was carrying on so about me that all at once my head commenced to spin like a top. I felt plumb awful standing there while everyone bragged on me.

"Look at his clothes!" one of the kids stopped running around the room long enough to say, and he stood staring and pointing at me. The other kids stopped running too and stared.

"Did you get burned?" another kid asked.

"Aw, naw . . ." I muttered.

Next thing I knowed, the menfolks was coming up to shake my hand like I was a grown-up, just like them, and Miz Hazelton handed me something lumpy in a folded napkin and said, "I reckon you can guess what this is, Arnold."

I looked down at the napkin feeling filled up to my hairline with red speckles of embarrassment. I never expected folks to be at home waiting for me and thanking me for saving the life of the meanest old buzzard in nine counties! I never expected that and I sure didn't expect Miz Hazelton to give me a piece of Daphne's left-over chocolate walnut birthday cake with a whole two inches of icing on it.

"T-thank you, ma'am," I told Miz Hazelton as I took the cake.

"Go out in the kitchen and have yourself a big glass of milk with it, Arnold," Ma said with a beam on her face like the rays of the sun had caught her there.

I was glad to get out of that room. If them folks knowed how I would of ruther run away from that shack than to go into it and pull old man Hooker out, if they knowed how I'd hung back and not wanted to save his rotten old hide, if they knowed all that, I reckon that front room would of been mighty vacant and silent.

In the kitchen I sat down at the table and opened up the napkin Miz Hazelton give me. Some of the icing from the cake was stuck to it and I took my finger and scraped it off and put it into my mouth. It tasted so rich and good, I could almost forget about old man Hooker and how I hated him. I took a big bite of the cake, hoping it wasn't the part where Gussie had stuck the jax ball in!

"I had Mama save that piece of cake just special for you, Arney."

I knowed that voice and I looked toward the door just as Daphne come bounding into the kitchen with her big wide smile and her cheeks pushed up. I hunched over, chewing slowly and looking up under my eyebrows at Daphne. She went to the icebox and got the jar of milk out and poured it into a cup, brought it to the table and set it down in front of me. Before I could lick the icing off my fingers, she was leaning close against me whispering, "I'm so proud of you, Arney. Ain't no other boys I ever knowed in my whole life brave enough to go through a real fire and save a life. And know what?"

I near about choked on them cake crumbs listening to Daphne talk like that.

"I'm going to give you something to show you how proud I am of you," Daphne went on, leaning even closer to me and getting her lips all puckered up.

"Oh, no you ain't!" I yelled as I tossed the cake down, jumped up and beat it out the back door.

I'd of ruther kissed a hornet than to of let Daphne Hazelton kiss me! I'd of ruther walked barefoot through a field of ten-inch-high sticker patches, been chased by a bull, et worms! Anything! No sir! I sure didn't want Daphne Hazelton kissing me! Looked to me like any girl with even half the brains she was born with ought to know that by now.

Chapter

12

You might know where old man Hooker ended up after his place caught on fire. Yep. Right in my own house! And if that wasn't bad enough, he ended up in *my own bedroom*! That was what my pa would of called "adding insult to injury."

Well, by the time that happened, I was beginning to think the old devil hisself had it in for me, the way he wouldn't let old man Hooker die and the way he always put me in the path to save his ornery old neck and now, to set him right down in my own house! Seemed like I couldn't get away from him no matter what I done.

The day that I come in from digging Granny's flower patch and heard Sal fussing with Ma is how I found out about it.

"How could you do it, Ma?" Sal was saying in a high, excited voice that sounded like she might go to crying at any minute. "How could you let that mean old thing come here to live with us?"

I stopped stone still on the porch to listen.

"We got Granny Stallcup here, ain't we, Sal? We took her in, didn't we?" Ma asked in a gentle voice.

"That's different," Sal said. "Granny's good to everyone and Tice Hooker never did a good thing that I ever heard of. He don't even show up in church unless there's going to be a picnic or a dinner at someone's house and he can get a free meal!"

"Hush that kind of talk, Sally!" Ma said.

"Where's he going to sleep?" Sal went on.

"In Arnold's room."

When I heard that I busted through the door like a cyclone! I couldn't hardly believe such a terrible thing could happen to me. Ma and Sal looked up when I come spinning through the door.

"Arnold?" Ma said, raising an eyebrow at me.

I looked at Ma, at her dark eyes and short, curly hair that always had little stray hairs falling into her face, and at her mouth that I never heard a cruel word come out of. Her face was pure kindness, just like her heart was. How could she of done this to me, I wondered.

Sal was setting dishes on the table and suddenly she plinked a plate down hard. It made a PING sound, wound in a circle, round and round, and thumped still.

"Watch what you are doing, Sally," Ma reprimanded her. "Ain't no reason to get so upset just because Tice Hooker is coming to live with us. It won't be for long. Just until he can get his shack built back."

Build his shack back! He was going to build on that half-burned-out old hulk of wood? I had been sure he was going to move completely away from Weedpatch and I'd be shut of him for good! It was what I'd hoped and prayed for. I couldn't believe what Ma was saying. My lips commenced to shake in a fury.

"That old buzzard! That nasty, mean old . . ."

"Arnold!" Ma cried over my words.

"He's as mean as the devil!" Sal put in, glaring at Ma. "Hush that kind of talk, both of you. What kind of person would I be, working in the church and trying to live a good, decent life, and to raise you two young'uns that way, if I didn't take in a soul that was in need and had no other place to go? How could I go to church on Sunday and . . ." Ma started and I cut her off.

"What about all the other folks in town? What about Miz Becker and Miz Hazelton and all them others? Why can't one of them take him in?" I was shaking all over, I was so dad-blamed mad at the thought of having to live under the same roof with that old man. I was near about in a yelling frenzy.

"They was others who wanted to help, but Tice wanted to stay here because we are closer to his place and he can walk over there every day and begin to build on his shack," Ma said in soft voice that made me feel ashamed that I'd spoken so harsh to her. "You children can sacrifice for a little while. It won't hurt neither one of you."

"What about Granny?" Sal asked as she plunked herself down in a chair at the table.

Sal no more than got the words out than Granny was in the doorway of her storage-room bedroom with the curtain-blanket lifted up and saying, "I been having to make adjustments all my life. I reckon I can adjust to this too." But the look on Granny's face said she'd hate to worse than anything.

"If Granny can do it, so can you young'uns," Ma said like she was relieved Granny had spoke up the way she done. "Now, let's all set down at the table and have our supper before it gets cold."

I washed up and sat down at the table feeling like this would be my last supper in peace and comfort for a mighty long time. And I was right.

Seemed like the whole day and night whirled away faster than usual and then it was the next day and old man Hooker was coming down the road toward the house, pulling a big old blanket filled with his belongings. The dust stirred up around the blanket as it scooted along and made a smooth path down the middle of the dirt road. Buck and Bill set up a howl soon as they seen the swirl of dust and realized it was old man Hooker coming in our direction. I'd already got them tied to the porch post like Ma had me to, knowing they'd have a fit over the old fool. Their howls and barks and snarls could be heard in the next county, the way they was carrying on.

When old man Hooker reached the gate he looked up and yelled, "Shut them dad-blasted hounds up!"

Without me even thinking, my chin went up and out in a defiant way at the old man. Reckon he thought he owned the world, now he was getting to move into my house and my bedroom and I'd saved his no good hide twice! I was winding up into a whirl of passion, ready to jump at him, but Ma come to the door and looked out at me and Buck and Bill and said, "Arnold, make them hounds hush."

When she seen old man Hooker coming through the gate, she opened the door wide and waited for him to make his way across the yard and up to the porch, dragging that dirty old blanket. He took his good time about it and dropped the blanket near the steps.

"Arnold, pick up Tice's belongings and take them into your room," Ma told me.

I shrunk back and hung on to Buck's neck. Touch that

old man's grubby things! Put them in my room! Shut up the hounds! Looked like I was in for the worst time in my life, except for the time Pa was killed. Looked like winter was going to begin the minute I entered the house behind that old coyote! Summer was over even though it had just started. I reckoned I'd never see the sun shine again.

All the time I was dragging his old things into my room I was huffing and puffing out a long story to Pa inside my head. I was telling him all about what Ma was making me do and about that mean old Tice Hooker and how he was bound and determined to make me so miserable I wouldn't even want to live no more. But as time went on, I wasn't the only one made miserable by him.

Ma was in a fix just trying to keep that old man happy with the food she put on the table and the way she cooked it. If she fried pertaters, he wanted them boiled. If she put turnip greens before him, he wanted okra. Half the time he complained because everything was too salty and the other half because it wasn't salty enough. I could tell Ma was getting mighty nervous just having the old coot around. And she kept me coming and going, trying to keep Buck and Bill quiet, and it looked like Gobble hated Tice Hooker about as much as I did. Each time he seen the old man start out the front door and head across the porch, he'd fly like the wind from around a corner, making a shrill ruckus that would make old man Hooker jump and commence to cuss a blue streak.

"When you going to kill that old turkey?" he asked Ma one day.

"She ain't!" I said real quick.

"Gobble is our pet," Sal spoke up.

"When you going to kill that old turkey?" old man Hooker repeated, louder this time.

We was in the kitchen and Ma was at the stove dishing up plates of vegetable stew. She looked around at old man Hooker and said, "Gobble is the young'uns' pet. We don't plan to ever kill him."

"Humph!" old man Hooker snorted. "Turkeys is to eat, not keep as pets, same as young'uns is to be seen and not heard!"

Young'uns! My dander shot up in a fury! I was thirteen and Sal was almost twelve and we wasn't no young'uns!

Me and Sal looked at each other, then at Ma who appeared at a loss for words. But finally she said, "I've always encouraged Arnold and Sally to be heard as well as seen, Tice."

"Humph!" old man Hooker snorted again with a disgusted look on his face.

Me and Sal smiled at each other, glad that Ma had took up for us. But it wasn't long before Ma made me take Buck and Bill down to the barn and keep them there permanent, due to the old man's complaints. It didn't seem right or fair that Buck and Bill couldn't have the run of the place no more. "One of these days," I told them in a private whisper, "we won't none of us have to put up with Tice Hooker no more. I'll see to that." I was seeing what I had to do real clear. They both nuzzled in close to me and commenced to whine a little, just like they knowed exactly what I was talking about.

Chapter

13

U se to be summer rushed by so quick after school was out, I couldn't even remember where it went. Sal and me would both get real lazy with sleeping late most mornings and staying up way after dark most evenings, playing hide and seek with Gussie and Travis and the other kids that hung around our place. But what used to seem like the shortest days turned into the longest days I ever lived, with old man Hooker under our roof and sleeping in my room to boot. It wasn't so bad when he was up at his place working on the old shack, or when Gussie and Travis and me was down at the creek fishing off our inner tubes or looking for worms. But when I come in at night there he'd be, setting in Pa's own chair, fussing about something or making some kind of complaint about something else. There wasn't no way on earth to please him.

When Ma took Sal to birth Miz Sullivan's baby, he put up a protest like he was a doctor or something. "Young'uns don't know nothing about such matters!" he grumbled.

"Sally helped me birth one of the James's babies and the

last Bilbow baby that come in the spring. She's a big help to me, Tice," Ma said straight out to old man Hooker. But it was plain he didn't think a kid could do anything.

Soon as Ma and Sal left, old man Hooker jerked hisself up out of Pa's chair, still grumbling, and hustled out to the porch where Gobble was stalking around. Soon as Gobble seen him, he shrieked and old man Hooker howled and they both took off of that porch in a shot. I sat on the floor and laughed till my belly ached!

It got to where Granny stayed in her room so long at times, it looked like she wouldn't never come out. Then one day near the end of summer when old man Hooker wasn't around, Ma went and pulled back the blanket over Granny's door and said, "Granny, you ought not to confine yourself to your room like this."

"Well, I reckon you're right, Cora. I ain't been right with the Lord neither, ever since you took in Tice."

"I had to take him in, Granny. I know it's hard on you, but there wasn't no one else who really wanted to do it and he wanted to come here. It's set a plague on us all having him here, but I couldn't *not* take him in."

"Of course you couldn't, Cora. And I'm going to get right with the Lord and speak civil to Tice even if it kills me!" Granny's blue eyes was snapping with determination when she said that.

That evening Granny come out of her room and helped Ma get supper ready and the dishes set on the table. She seemed to of got so right with the Lord that she took up to singing out loud and clear. "Wheeen the roool is called up yooonderrr . . . wheen the roool is called up yooonderrr, I'llll be there . . ." The sound of her voice mixed with the smell of the cornbread baking in the oven and made the whole kitchen come alive.

All at once old man Hooker looked up from the table where he sat all hunched over, and snarled, "Can't there be no peace in this house? If it ain't young'uns yelling, it's dogs barking and a durned fool turkey gobbling! Now it's an old woman singing!"

Granny stopped singing and looked like she'd been hit right across her face. Ma turned around from the stove and said in a voice that she tried to make sound pleasant, "Well, I think it right nice to hear a hymn just before we set down to the table."

All at once Gobble took flight from the yard and flew up on the back porch and started walking around making his loud GOBBAGOBBAGOBBA noise.

"Listen to that! It ain't civil to have a durned turkey running around free like that! It ought to be killed and et," old man Hooker exploded.

Me and Sal exchanged a look and when I looked back at old Tice Hooker I narrowed my eyes, mashed my mouth down hard and folded my fists in my lap under the table.

"Arnold, go get Gobble off the porch," Ma told me.

"Gobble's always been allowed on the porch, Ma," I spoke up in protest, but Ma give me a look and I got up and went outside and coaxed Gobble down off the porch and around to the side of the house.

"You spared the rod and spoiled them young'uns, Cora Burdette!" I heard old man Hooker say as I jumped down off the porch.

"Now, Tice, you hadn't ought to say such things to Cora. She's done a fine job in raising these two young'uns all alone," Granny come to our defense mighty fast and sharp.

"That boy!" Tice Hooker snarled.

It was plain now that he hated me as much as I hated him! Only, I didn't know *why* he hated me. Maybe it was because I saved his old durned fool neck them two times. Maybe that was it. Maybe he realized he wasn't fit to live with humanity and hated me for saving him from the peace of not having to live with hisself. I didn't even know why he hated Buck and Bill and Gobble. But, I reckon the truth of the matter was, he had a deep down hatred for everyone.

At the side of the house I dropped to my knees in the dirt and hugged Gobble's neck. He stood still and blinked his eyes at me. I could tell he was mighty put out over having to stay off the porch. I patted down his feathers and told him not to worry. "It won't be for very long, ol' pal. It won't be much longer at all . . ." I said as I stood up and watched him raise his wings and fly across the yard.

I went back inside the house and sat down at the table. Ma carried the platter of turnips to the table and set it down. Then she turned to Granny, who was standing close to the stove with her mouth all pursed up.

"Come and set down, Granny, and we'll have grace," Ma said.

Granny turned and give old man Hooker a disgusted look, then she come to the table, sat down, and looked right down at her plate.

"Arnold?" Ma said, waiting for me to say grace.

I didn't want to say grace. If it hadn't been for old man Hooker, I would of been glad to thank the Lord for all the food and everything else. But with him moving in and staying, what did I have to be thankful for?

Granny must of understood how I felt because she shoved her glasses back on her nose and snapped, "I think it would be right nice if *Mister* Hooker said grace."

We all looked at the old man. He was peering up at us from under his eyebrows and sputtering like Vesper Gene DeGoff's old pickup when he's trying to get it started. You sure could tell he didn't want to say no grace.

"I reckon *Mister* Hooker has plenty to be thankful for," Granny went on. 'I reckon he'd like to not only thank the Lord for all the fine food you been setting out each and every day for him, Cora, but for the roof you put over his head in his time of need and for Arnold saving his life."

Me and Sal exchanged a little kick under the table and Sal brought her hand to her mouth to cover a giggle.

"Well . . . well . . . I . . . I . . . ." Old man Hooker sputtered and we all stared at him.

"All you got to do, Mr. Hooker, a grateful man like you, is thank the Lord," Sal said with pure devilment in her gray-blue eyes.

The old man looked like he was about to explode. His lips commenced to move a mile a minute in them sputters. It was plain he'd never said grace in his life!

"Pass them turnips!" he blasted out suddenly.

Ma, looking embarrassed and uncertain, picked up the bowl of turnips and handed them to old man Hooker. It was the first time I could ever remember not saying grace at the table before we et.

That evening Ma and Granny went to set out on the porch while Sal cleaned up the kitchen and I went to feed

Buck and Bill. Old man Hooker had already gone to my room to go to bed. From down in the yard I could hear the steady squeak-squeak of Ma's old rocking chair as Granny moved back and forth in it and Gobble making a few noises as he settled down in Ma's flower bed, getting ready to go to sleep. The night was still a deep summery blue with just enough stars and moon so's a feller could see everything. There was the gentle swish-swish of the branches of the pepper trees and crickets near the house kept up a steady chant. I laid out the scraps from the table, what there was of them, for Buck and Bill and set down to look up at the stars.

"Granny, in town today, I heard tell that Amelia is coming back," Ma said, and I looked around at the porch.

"Tice's girl? That poor child! Why do you reckon she'd want to come back here, Cora?" Granny asked, and the rocking chair stopped squeaking as she leaned toward Ma who was setting in a straight-backed chair close by.

"Edward Martin has been sent overseas and they say he ain't got no family of his own for Amelia to stay with," Ma answered with a big sigh.

"I'd never come back," Granny said with a firmness in her voice.

"Amelia's in a family way, Granny. There's nothing else she can do."

"Lord save us!" Granny exclaimed, and she leaned back and commenced to rock again.

Amelia coming back! And in a family way. I knowed what *that* meant. It meant old man Hooker's daughter that he throwed out was going to have a baby.

"Where is she going to stay, Cora?" Granny asked be-

89

tween squeaks of the rocking chair. "Even if Tice's place wasn't burned out, he'd not let her come back."

Ma sighed so big and so loud I could hear her all the way down in the yard. "I don't know, Granny," she said, but I could tell from the sound of her voice that she was thinking hard on where she could make a place for Amelia Hooker Martin in our house.

Chapter

14

I knowed something was wrong the minute I opened my eyes. I raised up in bed and looked out the winder. The sun was coming up like a red ball and the roosters was crowing, announcing that the day was ready to begin. I could hear the chickens scratching around in the yard and Buck and Bill snorting and yapping at each other. Everything seemed the same. But there was something missing. I could feel it way down in my bones where Pa always said a feller was apt to feel things first when he couldn't explain a strange sensation.

I took a look down in the floor at old man Hooker laying on his pallet Ma fixed for him. He was sleeping sound as a man who never done a wrong deed in his life. Curled up in a tight little ball the way he was, with his head resting in the crook of his arm, he looked a lot smaller. More like some innocent little kid than the mean old sidewinder man that he was. I looked away and rubbed my eyes, tossed back the covers and got out of bed. That strange silence of something I couldn't figure out was as heavy in my ears as if it was roaring. *What* was it?

I went to the winder and looked out again. Everything was just like it always was early in the morning when the sun first comes up and all the trees and flowers and bushes are still damp from the nighttime dew. There was Buck and Bill laying down with their necks flat on the ground and their paws stuck out in front of them, looking like they was getting ready to doze off. The chickens was walking all around pecking at the ground, going in and out under the house. Off in the distance, I could hear Jeb Worth's cows putting out a call to be milked and, from the kitchen, Granny humming and clanking the coffee pot on the stove. Ma was in Sal's bedroom trying to wake her up. Everything was the same as always. Even Ma having to raise her voice to Sal to get her out of bed was the same. But that missing thing got louder and louder in my head.

I scratched my head and rubbed my eyes and ran them over the yard again and, there, next to one of the big pyrocantha bushes, laying in Ma's flower bed, was Gobble. I stared hard at him, waiting for him to make a move, to get up and raise his wings and go to making his shrill noise and fly around. But he was stone still. His feathers was all spread out and his long neck laid in the blue morning glories. His eyes was closed. All at once it come over me like a fierce explosion. Gobble was dead!

I took off in a run from my room, not even stopping to put on my clothes, just streaking through the house in my long-handle longhandles. As I beat a path through the kitchen, Granny spun around from the stove with a surprised look on her face.

"What in the world!" she exclaimed, as I dashed through the door and down the back steps. I was across

92

the yard and up to the flower bed where Gobble laid, faster than a streak of lightning. I bent down on my knees and studied Gobble close. He was dead, all right. And there was dried blood on his neck, all over his comb and sticking in his beautiful feathers. A big lump come into my throat and stuck there. I reached out and touched the feathers that was hard with the dried blood. I moved them a little this way and a little that way and that was when I seen the mean-looking hole in Gobble.

"No! No!" I cried and I laid my head down in Gobble's feathers, on the big lump of his back, and pretty soon I could smell the dust swirling up from the feathers and it made tears come to my eyes.

"Arnold! What is it?" Ma was calling out to me from the porch, but I couldn't raise my head or look around. I just wanted to lay there with my head in old Gobble's feathers. But pretty soon I heard Ma next to me. She leaned down beside me and touched my shoulder with her hand.

"Gobble's dead, Ma," I managed to say, but the words that come out didn't sound like mine. They was all raspy like I was some old man that wanted to die, but couldn't.

Ma reached down and touched Gobble's feathers where the hole was and made a sharp noise of surprise. "Who could of done this, Arnold?" she whispered in anger.

I raised my head and looked back toward the house with the passion of hatred throbbing in my heart and mind. It was a passion so savage that it made my whole body tremble and my insides quake like I was a volcano getting ready to erupt and everybody had better get out of my way!

"Don't you know, Ma?" I said in that same raspy voice.

Then I looked at Ma and they was a horrified expression on her face.

"No, Arnold!" she said, and she looked straight into my eyes like she knowed what I was thinking and who I was thinking about.

"Yes, it was!" I said in an even voice.

"No!" Ma repeated with a determined sound. "It had to of been some stranger who didn't know Gobble was a pet or someone with a gun that misfired."

"Don't make excuses for him!" I shouted in the fit of my passion, and I jumped up and started racing across the yard to the house. I could hear Ma behind me, and the chickens clucking and scattering out of the way.

"Don't do it!" Ma shouted. She knowed I was after Pa's hunting rifle. She knowed it the way she always knowed things that took others a long while to figure out. She knowed I was going to kill that no-good Tice Hooker that shot and killed Gobble!

I blasted through the door of the house, almost knocking Granny over as she was on her way across the room with a cup of coffee in her hand. She went spinning around again and gasped as Ma ran in the door behind me. I reached the fireplace where Pa's rifle hung over it and my arm shot up to yank it down from the hooks when, all at once, Ma's hand was on my arm jerking it back. She grabbed both my hands and held them so tight I couldn't move them and looked me square in my eyes.

"Arnold Burdette, *how dare* you think to do such a vicious act against another human being! Your daddy would be fierce ashamed of you if he knowed what was in your mind! He would *disown* you as his son if he knowed such thoughts was a part of you!"

94

I looked down at my bare feet with my toes all dirty from the wet earth and the dark smudges on the knees of my white longhandles and, all at once, I felt cold. I started to shiver and sink toward Ma. She let my hands go and pulled me close. I could feel her hand in my hair and the smell of her close when I took in my breath.

"I know you're hurt inside, Arnold, and I can feel your pain just like it was my own, but you can't do no harm to Tice Hooker. Gobble was your friend, but he wasn't no human being. Besides all that, you ain't got no proof of who killed that turkey."

"I got the proof of my feelings!" I cried. "I got the proof of my insides! He's the only one around who wanted Gobble dead!"

"I heard a gunshot last night," Granny said softly from the kitchen doorway. I looked around. She was standing there in her flour-sack apron and faded dress, and her coffee cup was in her hand. "I heard it along about midnight and I thought it to be someone over to Jeb Worth's place. They is always out in the scrub shooting at something."

I shook my head fiercely. "Wasn't no one over to Jeb's, Granny."

"Maybe it was," Ma said.

"I heard the shot too. It was real close," Sal said, coming into the room. "It woke me up. Jeb Worth and no one else ever shoots close to our place."

Ma sighed. "Well, I reckon we'll ask around," she said.

"Don't have to ask no one," I cried.

Ma pushed me away from her and give me her sternest look. "You leave Tice Hooker be, Arnold! Do you hear me? You leave him be, lest the fire of damnation pay you a visit!" When Ma said that, I could see the fire already burning in her eyes. "Fact of the matter is," she went on, as she pushed the wisps of hair up and off her forehead, "Tice Hooker belongs to you now."

I drew back, filled with shock and disgust at what Ma said.

"I reckon that be true," Granny said with a deep sigh. "You done saved his life. That means the Lord has give him to you to watch out for."

I stomped my foot on the floor and shook my fist in the air. "What?" I bellered, and the sound of my voice went all through the house.

"If you save a life, it means the Lord made you keeper of a soul. It's a special responsibility, boy. Not many folks is privileged in such a way," Granny went on.

"NO!" I shouted. "I wouldn't of saved that mean old fool's life for nothing in the Lord's whole kingdom! I wouldn't of saved his nasty old soul if the Lord hisself come to me and told me to! I wouldn't of . . ."

Ma took my face in her hands and tilted it toward her. "But you *did* save his life, Arnold Burdette. You did and now don't you do no harm to what the Lord give you to protect."

Protect! The Lord *give* to me! I could of thrown up every toenail I had! I could of thrown up my whole insides right out of me, to hear them words Ma said! I could of took that gun of Pa's and blasted that mean old man's brains right out of his head while he laid on the floor in my room. I could of done it, but I didn't.

Ma and Granny kept up talking about how it was some stranger that shot Gobble accidentally and how Tice Hooker might be mean, but he'd never do a thing like that.

It made me want to scream just to hear them talk on and on about it. I couldn't even think of that old man without my blood boiling over and wanting to foam right out of me!

A little later, me and Sal carried Gobble down to the side of the barn that faced where the sun come up and where there was peacefulness in the trees. Gobble would like it there. They was plenty of insects that he always liked to eat and there was a coolness and softness in the earth all year round.

Sal sat down on the ground with her head bent and resting on Gobble as I dug a deep, wide hole to place Gobble in. "You know he done it," I said as I put my foot on the shovel and pushed it into the ground. "You know he did, Sal." I couldn't hardly stand to look at Gobble. He looked so alive, just like any minute he'd go flying across the yard and shrieking out his high-pitched beller.

"I reckon," Sal said solemnly, raising her head and rubbing at the tears in her eyes. "I'm sure going to miss old Gobble."

After I got the hole dug, we put Gobble down into it as gently as we could. Sal patted down his feathers one last time and looked up at me. "You reckon Gobble would mind if I pulled just one feather out of him to keep, Arney?" she asked.

"Won't hurt him now," I said. "He couldn't feel it if you was to pick him clean."

Very carefully, Sal pulled a bright, beautiful feather out of Gobble's side and kissed it. Then she touched it down lightly on Gobble's head. "Good-bye, Gobble . . ." she whispered, and lifted the feather away.

Sal moved back and I started shoveling the dirt over Gobble. "Dust to dust," I said.

"And ashes to ashes," Sal said as she stood on the other side of the grave.

I let the last shovelful of dirt fall on top of Gobble. He was all covered. Only a few feathers pushed up through the dirt.

"Amen," Sal said.

I took the shovel and patted the earth down over Gobble and leaned the shovel against the barn. "Well," I said, "I reckon we ought to have some silence now, like Preacher Jessup asks when someone dies."

"I reckon," Sal agreed, and we folded our hands and bowed our heads and closed our eyes and was quiet in our thoughts and feelings.

When I looked up, first thing I seen was old man Hooker out on the back porch of the house gulping at a cup of Ma's coffee like he owned the place. A fierce, savage hatred coursed through me. I narrowed my eyes over him. It was the meanest and worst hatred I'd felt for that old man so far. *I'll get you now, you old devil!* I said way down deep inside me where I felt all the pain for Gobble. I'll get you someway, somehow. I'm going to kill you as dead as you killed poor old Gobble! *I swear I will!*

Chapter

15

For the next few days I waited my chance to get old man Hooker alone out in the scrub brush, in the foothills, near the creek, any place where I'd have him all to myself. I watched with a cautious study, waiting and biding my time. But it looked like I never could catch him in no deserted places. I hated that old man so much, I couldn't hardly stand to be near him no more or to have to put up with him in my own house. I'd hear him breathing in the night on the floor next to my bed, I'd hear him turn over or snore or cough and my feelings would ignite in me like his old shack catching on fire. I knowed as long as I lived, I'd never hate no one the way I hated Tice Hooker. That hatred took me over and lived in me like a second person under my skin.

Ma kept asking around if anyone had heard or seen anything on the night Gobble was killed. But no one except Granny and Sal heard a thing. That's because Gobble was killed in our yard. It soon dawned on me that, like as not, he was shot with Pa's own hunting rifle too.

School started again soon after Gobble was killed and

we had what Ma called a "sudden cold snap" because the temperatures had dropped so low. We had to pull on our sweaters and linger around the fireplace a few mornings. The change in the weather must of give old man Hooker a "sudden hunger snap" because he commenced to jaw about how it felt like fall in the air and how good a turkey would taste, stuffed and baked with cornbread dressing and sweet pertaters and all the trimmings. It near about made me want to throw up to hear him talk about eating a turkey after what I knowed down deep in my heart he'd done. Ma give him a hard look and told him we wouldn't be having no turkey this fall, not even for Thanksgiving. That we'd be doing good to have a hen and dumplings.

"Humph!" old man Hooker exploded. "We could of had a turkey right now if them young'uns of yourn hadn't buried that durned bird that runned around here in the yard all the time! Turkeys is to *eat,* not keep for a danged pet!"

"We loved Gobble!" Sal spoke up, looking heartsick.

"We had him a whole year almost, until you . . ."

"That will do, Arnold!" Ma cut me off real quick.

Well, it might of done for Ma, but not for me!

The next morning, it being a Saturday, me and Sal was out in the back field chopping weeds when we seen Travis and Gussie sneaking around near the outhouse. I leaned on my hoe and watched them. They went behind the outhouse, which sat down below a sloping hill behind a clump of tall bushes, and stayed a few minutes, then they come running out real fast.

"Hey!" I yelled at them. "What you guys up to?"

They headed toward us, snickering like they had a big joke going on between them. Sal stopped chopping weeds and watched them approach us.

"Remember that dynamite me and Gussie found near the railroad tracks?" Travis asked. I nodded my head.

"We hid it behind your outhouse," Gussie said with a grin.

"Why did you do that?" I asked.

"My old man went sniffing around in the barn and near about come right up on it. I reckoned I'd better get it out of there, else he'd find it next time. He sure never would go nosing around your outhouse," Travis answered.

"We don't want your old dynamite behind our outhouse!" Sal said, blinking at them through the sun.

"Wait a minute, Sal," I said, and my mind was working a mile a minute. This was what I'd been waiting for! "I reckon you can keep it there," I told Travis. I turned to Sal. "Don't say nothing about this to Ma."

Sal threw down her hoe and started walking toward the house. "Oh, I don't care about that old dynamite! I'm going to get me a drink of water," she said over her shoulder.

"Me and Gussie is going down by the railroad tracks. Want to go?" Travis asked me.

"Naw," I told them. "I got to get these weeds chopped."

They turned around and started walking toward the road. My mind was working *two* miles a minute now! Ma had some matches in the matchbox behind the stove in the kitchen. I'd get a couple and . . . I knew old man Hooker went to the outhouse around eight o'clock every morning. I could . . . No! . . . Still . . . I reckon I had me a sip of Moonstruck's wine of evil during the night because, next thing I did was to put my hoe down and run up to the house, dashing around the side and into the front room.

Sal was on the back porch getting her drink of water and

101

I didn't want her to see me. I opened the front door and peered inside. I could hear Granny humming a hymn in her room and Ma in her bedroom sweeping the floor. I closed the door quietly and hurried into the kitchen as quick as a little mouse skittering across the floor. In the kitchen, I dug my fingers into the box nailed up on the wall behind the stove and got me out two long matches, stuffed them down into my pocket and hurried back out of the house. As I ran past the house toward the field, I could see Sal still on the back porch. She was fiddling around with her hair and not looking my way. I reached the field and beat it as fast as I could around behind the old outhouse. Just as I did, Sal come walking down the porch steps with her hair pinned up on top of her head. I had to hurry.

Travis and Gussie hadn't done a very good job of hiding the dynamite. No wonder Travis's Pa was always finding things he hid! I scooped the stick up out of the leaves that was supposed to be covering it and reached for the matches in my pocket. My fingers was shaking, I was so nervous. Just touching that dynamite reminded me of how dangerous it was.

It was near about eight o'clock and I knowed any minute old man Hooker would come marching out the back door of the house and head down into the field. I leaned around the corner of the old building and seen Sal swinging down into the field. Then I heard the back door to the house open and bang closed. It was the old man.

Quick as a flash, I lit the stick of dynamite and jumped out from behind the outhouse and leaped over the hill and back to where me and Sal was hoeing. I picked up my hoe and waited.

"What you breathing so hard for, Arney?" Sal asked me.

"I ain't!" I snapped, and I picked up the hoe and commenced to chop at the weeds. But all the while, my eyes was up and watching the old man heading toward the outhouse. He passed us a little ways off and went on over the hill. My heart beat faster than I could bang that hoe into the dirt! In my mind's eye, I could see the old fool being blown into smithereens. It give me a pure satisfaction. But it didn't last. Something inside me wouldn't let it.

Old man Hooker opened the door to the outhouse, went in, and banged the door shut. My breathing stopped. I shot a glance at Sal. She was frowning at me.

"What's wrong with you, Arney?" she asked.

My voice caught like a slammed door in my throat. I couldn't breathe! Only my feet could move! I felt them under me, running off down the hill! Suddenly my voice come back and it went to screaming wildly. "Tice Hooker! Tice Hooker! Come out of there! Come out!"

The door opened and old man Hooker peered out with a deep, puzzled frown on his old mottled face. I reached out and grabbed his arm and yanked him up over the hill and away from the outhouse.

"What the hell!" he bellered as he fought and kicked to get away from me.

Soon as we reached the field where Sal stood with her mouth hanging open and her eyes wide, the outhouse exploded, sending the old, warped pieces of wood flying in all directions. Old man Hooker jerked free from me and Sal screamed.

"Well, I'll be a monkey's uncle!" old man Hooker muttered with his eyes bulged out, staring at the wood pieces as they hit the ground.

I swallered and licked my lips and brushed my arm

across my face to clean the sweat off. From the house, I heard Ma calling out and Granny crying something. Buck and Bill was barking louder than they ever barked and the chickens was clucking and flying all around. It looked like Ma and Granny was both in a tizzy. When I looked back at the outhouse, it was plumb gone, blown away into nothing but burning, smoking planks of old splintery wood.

"What happened?" Ma yelled. I glanced around again. She was down at the old sagging fence where she always hung the wash, leaning on it and staring straight at me.

"The outhouse blew up and Arney saved Tice Hooker's life again, Ma!" Sal yelled back, and I turned and glared at her. *Saved* Tice Hooker *again*!

It struck me then, like I was just realizing what I'd done. I'd *saved* that durned old fool *again*! I'd set out to get rid of him once and for all and I'd saved him from my own plot to do him in! I commenced to tremble all over, feeling my whole body fill up with horror and disgust.

Old man Hooker jerked his arm from my grasp and stomped his feet on the ground, shouting, "The hell you say! Warn't *nobody* saved me!"

"Was too!" Sal said, giving old man Hooker a fierce look. "Arney saved you!"

Old man Hooker commenced to stomp away like he was so sick of the very sight of me and everything that had happened, he just wanted to get shut of me.

"That mean old ungrateful thing!" Sal said when he was a little ways away from us.

"Are you all right, Tice?" I heard Ma ask as old man Hooker swiped past her and headed around the house.

I looked at Ma and her eyes was boring right into mine.

104

I swallered and swallered, wishing I could wash down all the guilt and disgust inside me for what I'd done and what I *hadn't* done.

A little while later, after the wood from the outhouse stopped smoking, Ma and Sal and Granny went to digging around in it, pushing planks over with their shoes and bending down to turn pieces over with their hands. I watched them from my bedroom winder with my heart jerking and thumping. Suddenly Sal jumped up with something in her hand.

"Look, Ma," she said excitedly, showing Ma something. "Look what it says."

Ma and Granny both leaned over to inspect what Sal had in her hand. "It says 'dynamite,'" Sal said, and my heart stopped pounding and leaped right into my mouth!

Ma looked up toward the house and I jumped away from the winder. Did she suspect something, I wondered?

At the supper table that evening Ma said, "Wonder who could of put dynamite in our outhouse?" I glanced at Sal then looked down at my plate real fast and commenced to chew hard on my carrots.

"Travis and Gussie found dynamite down by the railroad tracks once," Sal said.

I looked up, practically choking on a slice of carrot. "They has been some mean old boys hanging around the railroad tracks," I said nervously. "Travis and Gussie seen them."

"Humm . . ." Ma said, studying me close.

"They looked mean enough to blow up a house!" I rushed on. Me and Sal exchanged a quick glance.

"Did you see them?" Ma asked.

105

I cleared my throat. "Well . . . er . . . no, but Travis and Gussie told me what they looked like. Mean as all get out, they said." I cleared my throat again. Oh, Lord! One lie to cover up another one!

"Well, we'll have to set about building another outhouse," Ma said, and I looked back down at my plate. "Whoever done it had better do some mighty tall praying tonight and think about going to Sunday school on Sunday."

"Amen," Granny said.

"The one that done it probably don't never even go to church," Sal said, and I looked up at her, feeling like I wanted to defend myself. But I caught myself just in time.

"When I find out who done it, I'll knock the hell out of him!" old man Hooker said, chawing at his mouthful of food.

"A man ought not to use language such as that at the supper table," Granny said, glaring at old man Hooker.

"Humph!" old man Hooker said back.

That night, after I'd got Buck and Bill fed, and was walking back up to the house from the barn, I seen Ma come out and set down on the porch steps. It was cool and the wind rushed down through the pepper trees making a loud WHOOSH sound. Ma had a sweater around her shoulders and pulled it up tight around her.

"Arnold," she said when she seen me walking toward the porch, "come and set here with me a minute."

I sat down next to her and she turned to study me like she'd done at the supper table. "What if Tice had been truly hurt? Or Sally or Granny or even you?"

Her eyes bored right into me, just like she knowed the

truth of what I'd done. I wanted to tell her I wouldn't of hurt her ner Sal ner Granny for anything in the world. I wanted to tell her things was set up so's no one but old man Hooker would get blowed away. But I just hung my head. I reckon she knowed I was guilty, all right.

Ma ran her hand over the top of my head. "Well, the important thing is that you saved Tice."

I couldn't tell Ma, neither, that the important thing was that I *didn't* let the old fool get what he deserved.

"You know, Arnold," Ma went on, and she pulled me close to her so that I could smell the supper she had fixed in her hair and in her clothes, "this is the second time you've saved the old feller's life."

Not to mention the time I pulled him out of the creek, I thought with bitterness. But Ma and no one else knowed about that time.

"It seems like fate is just against Tice mighty strong lately, what with the fire burning him out and all and now this. Arnold, I want you to promise me you'll watch out extry special hard for him from now on. He's old and friendless, and ain't a soul around who cares about him."

I commenced to boil inside. "It's asking too much, Ma. I can't keep a watch out for him," I said, and I pulled away from her.

"Have you forgotten what I told you about him belonging to you now?" Ma asked in a low, soft voice.

"No!" I blasted, mad as a hornet. "I don't want that old devil to belong to me! I just want to get shut of him! I want him out of my bedroom and out of our house and out of our lives! He don't belong here with us!"

"I'm ashamed that you feel that way, Arnold Burdette!"

107

Ma said with a stern look. "Your pa would have a fit if he heard you saying such things. It's our duty to help the needy."

"Pa don't know what an ornery old cuss Tice Hooker is! He don't know he killed Gobble! He don't know all the mean things he says and does!" My voice was shaking, I was so het up with emotion.

"We don't know that he killed Gobble," Ma said with a softer look on her face. But, seemed like I could tell that she *did* know, just as well as I did.

"How long do I have to put up with him, Ma?" I asked again, trying to control myself.

"It won't be much longer. You know Tice has been going up to his place every day, working on the shack. Soon as winter . . ."

"*That* long?" There was a good two months until winter.

"He can't work on the place in winter," Ma said. "Especially with no one to help him. Can't you imagine what a chore he has at his age, carrying wood and hammering nails?" Ma looked thoughtful for a minute. "Now, if he had someone to help him . . ."

I suspected right away who that "someone" was Ma was thinking about. I stood up and headed across the porch and ripped open the door. "Not me!" I cried. I went in the house and banged the door closed behind me.

Chapter
16

Well, you might know that "someone" turned out to be none other than me, after all. Ma wouldn't listen to my protests or how much I couldn't stand old man Hooker. All she could talk about was how it was my Christian duty to help my brother who needed help. Seemed like there was no way I could get around or under or over or away from helping that nasty old goat.

The first day I went to old man Hooker's place, he cussed me up one side and down the other, swearing he'd never let me hit a nail into his old shack.

"Ma sent me to help you and I got to help you, much as I hate to!" I stood off away from him and yelled at him. I despised the sight of him.

"Don't need your help!" he yelled back, stamping his foot into the dirt and gripping a plank of wood up tight to his side.

I glared at him, standing there holding a bag of nails in one hand and that piece of wood in the other, with his old suspenders drooping off his shoulders and his undershirt as filthy as his old pants was. "You think I want to help a mean old thing like you? You think I'd be here to do a thing for you if Ma hadn't made me come? Why, you ain't nothing but a *calamity* in my life, you old buzzard!"

"Get away from here!" he yelled, and he took the plank of wood in his hand and throwed it at me. I jumped back and the wood landed on the ground at my feet.

"If you ain't the durndest, meanest old fool in all the world, I don't know who is!" I yelled with my fists doubled at my sides. "I ain't never seen no one as low-down bad! You're so bad, the Lord hisself wouldn't even let you inside the pearly gates!"

"Ain't no pearly gates, you damned little numbskull!"

My mouth dropped open and I exploded inside like one of them bombs we dropped over Hitler. Numbskull! That mean old man had called me a numbskull! I knowed I was going to hit him then. I knowed I was going to do it right then and there! I took off, rampaging toward him like I was a bull ready to trample him, but as soon as I got to him, my hand ripped the bag of nails from him and, at the same time, I reached for the hammer laying on a turned-over washtub. I grabbed for a piece of wood and commenced to hammer it like hell's own fury, into the old shack. Each time I hit the nail I cussed under my breath and, all the while, beside me, jumping up and down like he was madder than all get out, Tice Hooker cussed me. The harder he cussed, the harder I hammered. The longer he cussed, the harder I hammered. He cussed and I hammered until he was all cussed out and I was all hammered out. By the time I was ready to leave, he was inside what there was of the shack, pretending to be busy at something. I tossed the hammer down and took off walking down the road, feeling weary and dog-tired.

110

A little ways down the road I met Moonstruck Mulligan. He come walking in my direction with his gunnysack tossed across his shoulder and his juice harp held up to his mouth. The music from the juice harp made a merry sound and floated all over the road. When we reached each other, Moonstruck dropped his gunnysack and commenced doing a jig while still playing on the juice harp. I watched him like he was some clown I'd seen in a circus once. When he finished his jig, he grinned. I couldn't grin back.

"You look like you done tasted the bitter wine of evil, boy," he said.

"I reckon you think it's easy to help an old devil that's worse than a hundred rattlesnakes and fifty yellerjackets and . . ."

Before I could finish, Moonstruck throwed back his head and laughed. "Love thy neighbor, boy, and do good to them that persecutes you."

"I don't want to love my neighbor and I wouldn't do good to that old mule if Ma hadn't of made me!" I blasted.

"As thou has done, it shall be done unto thee . . ."

"Ain't true! I've saved that old fool's life three whole times now, and here I am fixing on his old shack! Ma took him in and I had to tie up my hounds, had to bury my turkey that I know he killed. I have to sleep with him in my own room, set with him at the table and watch him eat up all the food like Ma cooked it just for him. And all this when he is too durned mean to live! He runned his own daughter off, threw Granny out of her home, chased my sister, killed Gobble, and sets up a fuss day and night in a house that ain't even his! The old sidewinder!" Things fell out of me in such a rush, my head was spinning.

111

"This too shall pass," Moonstruck said with a bright twinkle in his sharp blue eyes.

"How come you always quoting from the Bible? You don't do nothing but go up and down the road, playing on that old juice harp and toting around a sack of turnips to sell! You're as crazy as old man Hooker is mean!" Soon as I said that I wished I hadn't.

Moonstruck commenced laughing so hard I thought he'd explode. He bent over and slapped at his knees and cut into another jig, dancing like a fool in the dust and sucking on that old harp. He was crazy, all right. He danced a circle around me, kicking up the dust, making it swirl all around me, sending it up like a thick cloud over me. I watched him through the dust and, all at once, I commenced to cry. I couldn't stop. I was plumb wore out, bone tired and mad too. I lowered my head and stood there in the road as much a fool as Moonstruck Mulligan was crazy, crying like a big baby.

Pretty soon the music stopped and Moonstruck said, "That's what you been needing, boy. A good cry."

I put my feet in gear and took off running down the road. A little ways off, I looked back. Moonstruck was doing another jig and the dust was swirling all around him like a whirlwind.

Chapter

17

Me and Sal got us a Coca-Cola out of the cooler inside Vesper Gene DeGoff's filling station while Ma got gas put in the car. I'd been helping old man Hooker on his shack after school and on Saturdays, but this Saturday I was helping Ma with some things. She let me and Sal buy us a Coca-Cola for helping her.

Everything looked just the same at the filling station as it did when Pa was there. It still had two gas pumps and the big sign over the door that said "Red Crown Gasoline," and off to the side, next to the door, the sign that said "Zeroline Greases" was still there. So was the one on the other side of the door that said "Coca-Cola in Bottles." It seemed like Pa ought to be there pumping gas right along with Vesper Gene.

When me and Sal come out carrying the bottles, Miz Porter drove alongside the other gas tank and called out to Ma. They got into a conversation while Inez rolled down the car winder and said, "Hello, Sally. Hello, Arney."

Sal went up to the Porter's car and started talking to Inez. I hung back drinking my Coca-Cola.

"I'll be with you in just a jiffy, Miz Porter," Vesper Gene said to Miz Porter as he continued putting the gas into Ma's car.

"Have you heard about Amelia staying with the Pines?" Miz Porter called across to Ma.

"Why no, I hadn't. When did she get back?" Ma called back.

"Just a day or two ago. The poor girl is due to have her baby any time now. Edward Martin is still overseas. No telling when he'll be back."

Vesper Gene finished putting the gas in Ma's car and went up to get the money from her. "I'd like to see Amelia," Ma said after she paid Vesper Gene and thanked him.

"Can I do your winders for you, Miz Burdette?" Vesper Gene asked Ma as he pulled a rag out of his back pocket.

"Not this time, thanks, Vesper Gene."

"Yes, ma'am," Vesper Gene said, and he walked over to Miz Porter's car stuffing the rag back into his pocket.

"I'm thinking on having a baby shower for Amelia right soon," Miz Porter said to Ma.

"Oh, that would be nice," Ma said.

"I'll let you know when."

"Let's go now," Ma called to me and Sal, and Vesper Gene said, "Don't you young'uns get off with them Coke bottles. Not unless you pay a deposit."

I swallered my Coke the rest of the way down and Sal give Inez a drink of hers to finish it off. Then she told Inez good-bye and went to get into the car while I took the empty bottles back inside the store. When I come out, Miz

Porter was just pulling away and Inez called out to me, "Bye, Arnold!" and she smiled so pretty I had to look away. I give her a short, quick smile before I done it, though. Inez had the brightest teeth I ever seen. Ma said once that Inez Porter had a "dazzling" smile. And I reckon she did.

"Ma, are we going to the baby shower Miz Porter is giving Amelia?" Sal asked as we got on the road.

"I reckon we will."

"Oh, I want to make a little bonnet!" Sal said excitedly.

"I think that would be right nice, Sally," Ma said. "They is lots of leftover scraps and bits of lace and some ribbon in my sewing bag."

"Oh, I can't wait!" Sal almost sang. And, fact of the matter is, she *did* sing. She leaned back in the car and looked out the winder at the mountain and commenced to sing: "Brushy Mountain, Brushy Mountain . . . what secret do you knoooow? Brushy Mountain, Brushy Mountain . . . I think about youuuu wherever I goooo . . . Brushy Mountain, Brushy Mountain . . . way up so highhhh . . . Will I learn your secret by and byyyy . . . ?"

When Sal had finished, Ma said, "What a strange song that is, Sally." Then she changed the subject and said, "Jeb was over to the house today saying him and some of the other men would build us a brand-new outhouse."

I looked out the winder feeling the rush of guilt overtake me.

When we got home, Ma and Sal and Granny, all three, went to discussing what they would make for Amelia's baby. They started going through Ma's bag of scraps and looked like they never would calm down about what they was going to make. I went outside and sat down on the steps and looked at Buck and Bill tied up down by the barn. I never could look at them two hounds all tied up like they was criminals, without feeling my blood boil inside me. Finally, I got up and walked to the barn and laid down on the ground beside them and they commenced to nuzzle into me.

"Won't be long," I told them. "Won't be long and that old shack will be all built back and we'll be rid of old man Hooker for good. Then y'all can stay in the yard and come in the house just like you use to."

Pretty soon Sal come out on the back porch and looked around. When she seen me, she jumped off the porch and ran down to the barn and plopped down on the ground and commenced to scratch at Buck and Bill's necks.

"Was you really going to kill him with that dynamite?" she asked me.

"Who?" I asked, but I knowed who she meant, all right.

"I been wanting to ask you ever since it happened, but seemed like I never could get a good chance to." Sal sat up and looked right into my eyes.

"Keep it a secret, Sal," I warned her.

"If you mean from Ma, don't you think she suspects already? If you was going to kill him, how come you to save him at the last minute?"

I laid down flat on the ground and looked up into the sky. It was growing dark and soon the stars would be out. I closed my eyes and felt one of the hounds' tongues on my cheek.

"Ain't you going to answer me, Arney?" Sal asked.

"If I knowed, I'd tell you," I snapped opening my eyes. It sure made me feel uneasy to be asked a question like that. "I ought to be horse whupped for saving that old goat!" I added under my breath and Sal laughed.

"You ain't as mean as you think you are, Arney," she said through her laughter. Then she said, "Daphne was asking about you the other day when me and Inez seen her in town."

"Daphne's fat!" I said.

"But she has pretty clothes," Sal said with a longing sound in her voice. Then after a little she said, "Arney, I want a blue dress with a white collar on it that's made out of lace and a full, flouncy skirt on it with a ruffle that swings in a circle every time I turn around and a little velvet bow on it somewheres."

"You don't need no fancy dresses to make you pretty, Sal. But don't you worry. Someday you'll have nicer dresses than Daphne ever dreamed of having."

Ma called us in for supper and when we sat down at the table she told old man Hooker, "Tice, Amelia is back." She said it straight out, looking right at the old coot. Old man Hooker's mouth dropped open. If he'd had store-bought teeth, they would of fell right out of his mouth. After he got over the shock of what Ma told him, he exploded with a disgusted, "Humph!"

"Amelia is in a family way," Granny put in.

Old man Hooker's mouth dropped open again and cornbread crumbs went flicking out the corners. He commenced to cough and choke a little. But he was all right.

"Miz Porter is having a baby shower for Amelia and I'd like to take you to it," Ma said, and old man Hooker sputtered that corn bread in all directions.

"I ain't innerested in no baby!" the old goat managed to shout out of his stuffed mouth.

"But this is your own gran'child!" Ma said with a fierce look on her face.

"I ain't innerested! I done told you!" Tice Hooker barked, and Ma and Granny exchanged a look.

Chapter
18

The front room of the Porters' house was decorated with pink, blue, and yeller flowers from her garden, and a table with a pretty cloth on it held presents that was wrapped in colored paper with bright bows tied on them. There was a swarm of ladies sitting in print dresses with tatted collars, jabbering and gossiping like buzzing bees and, on the divan near a wide winder with white see-through curtains, Amelia sat with a great big belly that made her dress stand out like it was covering a watermelon. I felt plumb out of place until Travis walked through the front door looking as uncomfortable as I felt. He shot away from his ma as quick as a rabbit and went to hang around near the wall.

Ma and Sal and Granny went right up to Amelia and give her a hug and a kiss, and Granny sat down next to her on the divan. Ma went to talking to her standing up, and Sal took their gifts over to the table and set them down with the others. Ma had made two little gowns for Amelia's baby and Sal and Granny had made a dress and a bonnet. While they was getting occupied with Amelia, I sauntered over to Travis.

119

"I sure am glad to see you," Travis said with a glance around the room. "I was afraid I was going to be the only one here to stand out like a sore thumb."

"Only reason I come," I told him, "is because of Miz Hazelton baking one of her fancy frosted cakes."

"How come your outhouse to blow up like it done?" Travis asked, eyeing me.

"If you hadn't left that durned stick of dynamite behind it, it never would of," I said, and I looked away, letting him know I was finished with the subject.

Travis scratched his head and muttered something about how could a stick of dynamite blow up all by itself. Then he said, "You reckon we'll get some ice cream along with that cake?"

"Sure. Sal told me all about the fixings."

"Well, in that case, I reckon I can stand the doings."

I looked over at Amelia. She sure didn't look nothing like old man Hooker. She was as pretty as she always was, with big dark eyes and long dark hair that lay loose around her shoulders and fluffed in curls close to her face. But there was a sadness in her face that didn't use to be there. I reckon her husband being overseas in some strange country and her going to have that baby didn't make her feel too good.

The door opened and I looked around to see Gussie walk through it with his ma. Gussie had a mad expression on his face and swiped at his hair like he was slapping at something. Soon as he seen me and Travis, he come up to us and commenced complaining about having to be there.

"I don't give a durn about parties and babies!" he said disgustedly. His ma heard him and give him a threatening look and he give out with a big sigh and looked down at the floor.

"Well, there ain't nothing to do but stand here until the cake and ice cream comes," I said with a sigh of my own and looked across at Inez who was chattering with Sal and Daphne. Inez would draw anyone's attention, she was so pretty. They would look at Daphne for a different reason. It was her clothes that always made folks give a second look. I cut a look over at Sal. Her dress was faded, as usual, but it had nice puffed sleeves and a pretty bow tie at the back. I caught her eyes slip across Daphne's pretty plaid dress and I felt a sadness overtake me.

"Poor Amelia . . . Poor Amelia . . ." everyone seemed to be saying, and all of a sudden Amelia sat up stiff and straight and said in a stern voice, "I'm tired of being called 'poor Amelia!'"

"The ladies only mean to sympathize with you, dear," Granny said, patting Amelia's arm.

"I don't need sympathy," Amelia said. "Understanding, maybe. But not sympathy. Just because Edward is overseas and won't be here when our baby is born . . . well, I ain't the only wife this has happened to and, Lord knows, I probably won't be the last. And . . . and even though the war is over . . . well, our boys is still needed in some of them foreign countries. It's the folks in them bombed-out places that has lost their homes and everything they owned in the world that y'all ought to feel sympathy for. What I got to go through ain't nothing compared to that."

All the ladies started cooing and making little noises, and Granny patted Amelia's arm again and said, "Brave little Amelia."

"I ain't brave neither, Granny," Amelia spoke up real quick. "I'm just like all the other wives waiting for their husbands to come home."

I give Ma a look then. There was a time when she waited for Pa to come home. Her face showed the memory of that for just a second, then it disappeared. I looked back at Amelia, thinking about what she'd said about the people in them foreign countries losing their homes. Amelia didn't have no home, neither. I wondered where she was going to keep her baby after it was born.

Just like she was reading my thoughts, Miz Hazelton spoke up and said, "Your Daddy will soon have his place built back after the fire. I reckon you'll be staying with him until Edward comes home."

"Amelia can't stay with her daddy," Miz Pine spoke up. "He's done spread the word around how she can't stay with him. Not even when his place is finished."

"Why, land a'living, Audrey, watch what you say!" Miz Becker said with a frown at Miz Pine.

All the ladies commenced to cluck and mumble and Miz Pine said, "Amelia ought to know."

Amelia's face turned red. Her chin twitched and she placed her arms across her belly and sighed. Granny reached over and patted her again and Ma moved close and said, "Amelia, you're welcome to come and stay with me and the young'uns and Granny." Ma didn't mention old man Hooker.

Amelia looked up at Ma. "You done took in too many folks, Miz Burdette."

"The Lord always finds more room than I ever thought I had," Ma said with a kind smile.

You might know Ma would offer anything she had to someone in need.

Sal hurried away from Inez and Daphne where they had been arranging and rearranging the presents on the table. "You could sleep in my room, Miz Amelia," she said.

Amelia smiled at Sal. "Thank you, honey, but Miz Simpson has offered to let me stay with her up on Brushy Mountain and . . ."

"Brushy Mountain!" Ma gasped, and several of the ladies clucked their tongues. They all looked around at each other with heavy frowns.

"You can't go up there!" Miz Porter said, looking at Amelia like she'd gone and lost her mind. "Winter's coming on."

"The storms can be mighty fierce on that mountain in winter," Ma said.

"And it's too high up! There ain't no one around for miles," Miz Hazelton added.

"Who would help you if you needed help, Amelia?" Miz Becker asked.

"Reba Simpson ain't never around that old cabin much in winter," Miz Pine said before Amelia could say anything.

"It just ain't a good place to be," Miz Johnson added.

All the ladies stared hard at Amelia. "I don't mind the mountain," she told them. "Miz Simpson said she will be there and I'll have Edward's picture and his letters to keep me company." Then, like she wanted to change the subject, she looked across at me and said, "Arnold, folks has told me how you saved Daddy from the fire and that terrible explosion you had at your place. I reckon I owe you a great big 'thank-you' for that." She smiled at me and I could feel my face glowing hot. I didn't reckon Amelia would be thanking me if she knowed how much I hated her pa.

Like she just noticed us boys, Miz Porter said, "Inez, bring them boys over there by the wall some chairs to set in." Inez and Sal and Daphne took off into the kitchen and brought chairs out for us to set in. Daphne tried to edge Inez out of the way and give me the chair she brought, but Inez beat her to it. Daphne shoved her chair in Gussie's direction and flounced off in a huff.

"Sally, I never did forget the time you was a little bitty thing and was always singing your heart out. Do you reckon you could sing something now?" Amelia asked, smiling at Sal.

Everyone went to begging for a song then and Sal beamed out a look on her face that appeared as bright as the morning sun. "Go ahead, Sally, I'll play for you," Ma said, and she went to Miz Porter's pianer and struck a few bars. Sal follered her and turned around to face everyone. "Sing something special for Amelia," Ma whispered, and Sal cleared her throat and looked right at Amelia, who was still smiling, and commenced to sing.

"Oh . . . there's soon to be a baby booooorn . . .
And I hope it comes on Sunday Mooorn . . .
Everyone will shout and say, hip, hip, hooraaaayyy!"

Sal went on singing, making up new words as she went along, and Ma played chords on the pianer that somehow seemed to fit right in with the song. When she was finished, everyone clapped their hands and went to making them cooing sounds and sugary remarks they always do. Amelia's eyes filled with tears and she held out her arms.

"Sally, come here and let me give you a big hug for that song."

Sal went across the floor and got her hug and Miz Porter said, "This would be a good time to open your presents, Amelia."

Sal and Inez and Daphne took turns carrying the presents to Amelia, and every time Amelia opened one, all the ladies "oohed" and "ahhed" and carried on so that me and Travis and Gussie near about got disgusted-sick. After all the presents was opened, Miz Hazelton said, "I, for one, am ready for a little refreshment. How about you all?" I reckon Miz Hazelton was anxious for all them compliments to start rolling her way over that cake she'd brought.

Everyone agreed they was ready for the refreshments and Miz Hazelton got up and went to the kitchen and brought back her mouth-watering cake and set it on the table where the presents had been. The frosting was so white and so high on it, it looked like the snow at the very tippy top of Brushy Mountain in the deepest part of winter. Miz Hazelton went to cutting slices of it and putting them on little plates, and Sal and Inez and Daphne started passing them around with glasses of lemonade.

After all the ladies was served, the girls brought me and Travis and Gussie our cake and lemonade. Inez handed mine to me with a pert smile while Daphne tried to push her out of the way. When she seen she couldn't do it, she walked off in a huff again. Soon as I finished the cake, Daphne showed up with another piece for me. She smiled real big, now that she didn't have Inez in her way, and her cheeks went flying up.

"I could tell you liked that cake by the way you was eating it, Arney. My mama is teaching me how to bake just like her. One day I'll be baking and baking forever and ever. Mama says some young man is sure to want a fine girl that can bake like her," Daphne said, and Travis's mouth broke open in a laugh and his mouthful of cake went spewing in all directions. On the other side of me, Gussie tried not to laugh, but he looked like he was about to choke, holding it back. Daphne give them both a narrow-eyed glare and marched off.

After a little while Gussie said, "Here she comes again!"

I looked up and there was Daphne pounding across the floor with another piece of cake. Her cheeks was all puffed out and up with that smile of hers. "Ain't you finished with that cake yet?" she asked when she got to me.

I commenced to dig into that cake with my fork and to shovel it down like I was in some kind of contest. Soon as I got the last crumb down, Daphne snapped the plate out of my hand and slid the other one onto my lap. "That's more like it," she said, pushing her cheeks up in that smile. Then she turned and walked away.

Travis and Gussie snickered like two fools while I lapped up that cake. "Who do you like best, Arney? Old 'big cheeks' or her ma's cake?" Gussie asked with his eyes telling me he was holding back another big beller of a laugh.

I give him the narrow eye and hissed, "I ain't never liked no girl and I never will!" But it was a lie. I liked Inez Porter better than I even wanted to. I reckoned they knowed that, but they didn't say anything.

Seemed like not more than a minute passed when, here come Daphne again. Her eyes was set right into mine and I looked down real fast. When she got to me she handed me another glass of lemonade and said, "I thought you'd be wanting some more lemonade to wash that cake down with, Arney."

"Thanks," I said, and I wouldn't look up at her.

"You must be ready for another piece of Mama's delicious cake too," she said, and I started to protest, but I reckon my empty plate said I'd have another piece. Daphne took my plate and was off like a shot to get me another piece.

I looked over at Travis and Gussie's plates. They still had some cake left on them. I must be a bigger pig than that old sow of Charley Parlier's, I thought disgustedly. But I didn't have time to dwell on it because Daphne showed up with her pushed-up cheeks and another plate filled with an even *bigger* piece of cake. Wasn't I *never* going to get filled up? I wondered. But I cut right into the golden-yeller cake with the snowy-white frosting like it was a gift right out of heaven and had a blessing in every bite. After a while, though, I commenced to get a heaviness in the pit of my belly. With each bite I took from then on, that heaviness got deeper and deeper, until I felt like my belly was going to explode.

"What's wrong?" Travis asked, studying me with a close eye. "You look plumb green."

"He looks like he died and his ma forgot to bury him!" Gussie snickered and he slapped me on my back so hard I had to jump up.

The plate with the rest of the cake on it tumbled to the

127

floor and, as I ran for the door and blasted out of it with my hand over my mouth, I heard Ma calling out to me, "Arnold! What's wrong?" And behind her voice was them ladies clucking their tongues and buzzing like a barn full of bees and Granny's voice piercing through it all, "Lord of mercy, what's got into that boy?" The screen door banged closed with a loud THAWACK and Travis's voice cut through it saying, "He et too much cake!"

I beat it down the steps and around the side of the house and down a path to Miz Porter's garden. My hand reached out to a tree for support just as I throwed up in her flower bed.

Well, I reckon I was a pig, all right. And I felt like a fool on top of that. I pulled my handkerchief out of my pocket and swiped it over my face, sniffed hard and turned around, with my back against the tree. And there was Inez.

"Are you all right, Arney?" she asked gently. I looked down, I was so embarrassed. "Here," Inez went on, "put this damp cloth over your forehead. I had a feeling you might need it, as active as Daphne was in seeing you got filled up on her mama's cakes." At the sound of that word, I felt my belly jerk.

I took the cloth from Inez, sat down and leaned against the tree trunk and rubbed it across my face. It felt cool and soothing and I shut my eyes. I could feel Inez leaning close to me. She was closer than any girl had ever been to me except for Sal.

"It's awful easy to get carried away on Miz Hazelton's cakes," she said, and I could feel her breath in my face. I opened my eyes just as she kissed my cheek. She moved back then and said, "I think you'll survive, Arney Burdette."

We smiled at each other and I was ready to reach for her hand when a harsh sounding voice shot across the yard. "So here you are! Your mama says it's time for you to leave now, Arney."

It was Daphne with a frozen look on her face like she'd swallered an iceberg. Her hands was on her hips and her legs was squared off under her dress like she was getting ready for a fight.

I got up and helped Inez up and, glaring at Inez, Daphne said, "And *your* mama wants you to help her clean up the front room. Everyone is leaving."

"Thank you for telling me, Daphne," Inez said sweetly, and she raised her head into the air and walked ahead of me, past Daphne and up the path toward the house.

Daphne fell into step with me. "I hope you ain't mad at me, Arney. I mean, I hope you don't blame me for your getting sick." Her face was all thawed out now.

"Naw," I said, sniffing into my handkerchief.

"Well, good. Because I saved a real nice little piece of cake for you to take home."

I turned and looked at her and wondered if I really was turning green!

Chapter
19

It was winter now and Amelia had moved up on the mountain to Reba Simpson's place, and Ma and Granny never seemed to stop fretting about it. As big as Amelia was, Ma was worried that she was getting ready to have twins. "One baby or two, that mountain ain't a fit place for Amelia in her condition," Granny would say, and Ma would come right in with, "It ain't no place for no one in winter, Granny. How Miz Simpson can live up there in that cabin all alone, I'll never know." Then they'd go to sighing wearily and talking about other things. But they always come back to Amelia.

Soon Tice Hooker's shack was finished and he was ready to move back into it. The day he decided on going sure was a glorious day for me and Sal, and even Buck and Bill was near about to do somersaults all over the yard and in the house too. Only bad thing was, it was coming up a storm when the old coot figured he'd leave and it was already raining like it would never stop. I let Buck and Bill come in the house and lay down in front of the fireplace and old man Hooker near about had a conniption fit.

Soon as Buck and Bill finished turning in a circle like they always done before they flopped down, old Hooker was heading for the door with his dirty blanket full of his belongings tossed over his shoulder. Ma had offered to take him home and I was resentful of her having to do it in the rain.

"I'm ready to go," he informed Ma in a stiff voice while he give a mean backward glance at Buck and Bill.

"Just a minute, Tice," Ma told him impatiently as she pulled on her coat. "Now that your house is livable, I hope you'll let Amelia come back and live with you."

Old man Hooker turned at the door and faced Ma with a scowl. "The girl chose where she wanted to go! She chose to go off and hitch up with that soldier too!"

"You stubborn, cantankerous old fool!" Ma shouted and her eyes was snapping and crackling like fat in a hot skillet. "How long are you going to punish that girl? She's your own flesh and blood! Ain't you got no thought for your unborn gran'child?" Ma didn't mention that she suspected there might be more than one gran'child. She was shaking, she was so het up.

"Tice," Granny said from the kitchen doorway. There was a hard look on her face, but her voice was soft and serious. "Amelia has gone up to the mountain. It ain't a fit place for her to be. . . ."

"When it rains heavy, the mountain roads flood out and no one can get up or down them," Ma interrupted with a deep frown.

Old man Hooker sniffed loudly, shoved the door open and walked out. "I'll wait in the car," he threw over his shoulder to Ma.

131

"Oh! I ain't never seen no human as all-out stubborn as Tice is!" Ma exploded as she buttoned her coat.

"I told you that, Ma," I spoke up from the floor where me and Sal had laid down between Buck and Bill.

"That old man will get his comeuppance one day," Granny said with a smack of her lips.

"Well, I'll just have to go and get Amelia myself," Ma said, and she turned and peered out the winder at the rain. "I'll go tonight and bring her here. She can stay with us."

"You can't go up to the mountain in this storm, Cora!" Granny cried.

"I've *got* to, Granny! I can't take a chance on them roads flooding out in the next day or two. I'll get Jeb to take me up. His truck is as good as a mule in climbing them steep roads."

"Jeb's gone to Clement's Pond!" Granny said, and fear jumped inside me and commenced to grind away at me.

"Then I'll just have to go alone," Ma said with a determined look. "The sooner we get Amelia off that mountain, the better we'll all feel."

I thought of the black sky, of the rain washing down over the house, and the way the lightning split the darkness, making it look like the jagged edge of ripped-apart school paper.

"Soon as I take Tice home, I'll drive over to Jeb's and get his truck. He always leaves the key in it and . . ." Ma went on but before she could finish, someone ran up on the porch and started pounding on the door.

"Miz Burdette! It's me, Roy Crimp! Lula is about to deliver! She's in terrible pain!"

132

Ma frowned hard and hurried to open the door. Soon as she got it open, Roy panted out, "Can you come now, Miz Burdette? Lula's carrying on something fierce." Roy's face was all caved in with worry lines. He took off his hat and rain dripped from it.

"I'll have to run Tice Hooker home first . . ."

"But Miz Burdette, Lula needs you now!" Roy said with a passion. He had married Vesper Gene's use-to-be girl-friend and she was always driving past the filling station in Roy's car, waving at Vesper Gene. Looked to me like she hadn't made up her mind which one she liked the best, even though she did up and marry Roy.

Ma reached out and touched Roy's arm like she wanted to settle him down. "It will only take a little while to get Tice home, Roy. Lula's baby won't come that quick. The first baby always takes the longest to come. You'll find that out after you've had two or three."

Roy didn't say anything to that. He just rolled his hat round and round in his hands. Ma looked around at me and Sal and Granny.

"Ain't you going to be here for supper, Ma?" Sal asked with a big frown on her face.

"No, honey. You all go on and eat and go to bed just like I was here. I'll head over to Jeb's and get the truck after Lula's baby comes."

Granny went to the door and put her arms around Ma. "Don't seem right for a woman to have to go out in a storm like this, Cora."

"Don't worry, Granny," Ma told her. "A little storm never hurt no one. Besides, I've weathered bigger storms than this in my life." Ma looked at me and Sal and said,

133

"You both help Granny with supper and wash up the dishes after you eat."

Soon as Ma said that, a flash of lightning exploded like cannon in the sky and thunder crashed all around. "Lord of mercy!" Granny cried, touching her hand to her heart. "I ain't never seen such a storm!"

I got up and hurried to the door and watched Ma and Roy rush down the steps of the porch and across the muddy yard. Ma got into her car and Roy got into his and they both drove out of the yard with mud flying in all directions. Last thing I seen through the car winder before Ma pulled away was old man Hooker's skinny old head and his mashed down mouth.

While Granny stood at the stove stirring the gravy for supper and checking the biscuits in the oven, I closed the door and went back over to the fireplace, bent down and whispered to Sal, "Ma can't go up to Brushy Mountain and get Amelia! Not in this storm and not having to deliver Lula Crimp's baby. Remember how long it took the Parlier's baby to come? The roads is liable to be half washed away before she could even start up there."

"Pa wouldn't let her go if he was here," Sal said with a worried look as she scratched Buck's head. He snorted and sighed and blew the air out from his nose and little balls of dust went tumbling across the floor.

"That's right," I said, and I commenced to think hard.

Sal looked at me. "But there ain't no way we can stop her, Arney."

"Yes, there is," I told her, and I looked around to make

sure Granny was still at the stove. I could see her through the kitchen doorway. Sal sat up straight and looked into my eyes and I went on, lowering my voice even more. "What would Pa do if he was here, Sal?"

"He'd go up to the mountain and get Amelia hisself," Sal answered without no hesitation.

I nodded my head up and down. "And that's exactly what we're going to do."

Sal's eyes grew big. "We *can't* do that, Arney!"

"We *got* to, Sal. We could maybe get up there and be back before Lula Crimp's baby is even born." I glanced back through the kitchen doorway to make sure Granny hadn't heard us. She was still at the stove with her back to the door.

"But how?" Sal whispered, leaning close. Her eyes was still big and filled with fear now.

"Well . . . we'll borry Jeb's old truck, that's what we'll do," I whispered back. "It'll take the steep roads. Ma said that herself."

"Are you *crazy*?"

"Shush!" I cautioned her, and I bit down on my lip and checked again to see if Granny heard. She was sprinkling salt into the gravy and seemed occupied with her thoughts. I turned back around, narrowing my eyes at Sal and made my words firm. "We could have it back before Jeb misses it. Maybe even before he gets back from Clement's Pond. He hardly ever uses it. It just mostly sets there by the barn with the key rusting in it."

"We can't just *take* it!"

"Jeb ain't here to ask and we got to get Amelia down off that mountain before Ma's done birthing that baby. Ain't you got no feelings for Ma?" My voice had commenced to shake, I was so het up.

Sal looked worried. She reached down and scratched on Buck's ear for a while, then she said, "Well . . . if we went, what would we tell Granny?" I sighed with relief. At least she was listening to my plan. I reckoned I did the right thing in mentioning Ma.

"We ain't going to tell her, Sal. She'd just worry and try to stop us," I answered, and lowered my voice a little more. "We'll eat and wash up the dishes and claim to be wore out and sleepy. Then we'll go to our rooms, wait a few minutes, and sneak out the winders and meet in back of the house."

"But it's so cold and wet, Arney," Sal protested in a little whine with her face crumpled up.

"Put on your boots and coat! You've been cold and wet before!" I said, talking like I was Pa. I watched the guilt gather up on Sal's face. "Don't you think it would be wet and cold for Ma, and her already that way from running old man Hooker home and going to Roy Crimp's place?"

Sal put her head down like she was ashamed for thinking of herself before Ma. I was being harsh, but I couldn't give her a chance to back out. Finally she raised her head and said, "Well . . . I reckon I'll go." And relief ran all through me.

After that, Granny called us to the table and I give grace with me and Sal staring at each other across the table. When I'd finished, Granny went to passing around the food and me and Sal et in silence while Granny complained about the cold and rain. "Your ma will ruin her own health in helping others," she said, and I looked up from my plate at her.

"You're right, Granny," I said, and I looked at Sal. Granny had said the right thing without even knowing it.

"The sooner winter comes and goes, the sooner spring will be here," Granny said with a sigh.

"You're right about that too, Granny," I said.

When we finished eating, me and Sal got up to wash the dishes in silence and Granny went to set in her rocking chair beside the fireplace to read her Bible. We could hear the rain battering down on the roof and the wind rattling the slats of wood on the house and, every time the thunder and lightning roared and cracked, Buck and Bill raised their heads off the floor in front of the fireplace and whined a little. I sure wasn't looking forward to what laid ahead. When we was finished with the dishes, Sal commenced to yawn and told Granny she was going to bed. Granny looked up over her glasses and asked, "You going too, Arnold?"

"Yes, ma'am, Granny," I answered and I passed on by her and headed for my room. I left Buck and Bill laying in front of the fireplace. Now that old man Hooker was gone, they could stay in the house at night.

"Well, you young'uns rest well. Some folks sleep good with the sound of rain on the roof." After a little while Granny went to humming and I figured that was a good time to get out the winder. I was hoping Sal was thinking the same thing but, if she wasn't, I could tap on her winder to hurry her into gear.

"What a frieeend we have in Jesuuuuus . . . Alll our sins and griefs to beaaarrr . . ." Granny sang in a low voice.

I throwed on my jacket and my old knit cap and raised the winder just as Granny cut into the second verse of the hymn. The winder was low and I didn't have far to jump to the ground. I landed in a gush of mud with the rain and wind almost plowing me over. I got my balance and reached up to pull the winder down. When I looked around, Sal was standing there all bundled up in her coat and boots.

"Let's go," I told her and I took her hand and we started running across the field to Jeb Worth's place. The field was soft and muddy and filled with limp weeds that we buried under our boots when we stepped down on them. The sky was so dark and moody looking up above the mountain that it didn't look like no sky at all, but just a deep, black hole. Soon as we reached Jeb's fence and started over it, thunder and lightning commenced to rattle and crack. Sal looked back at me and I could see the fear on her face as plain as if it was daytime. She was astraddle of the fence and I had to give her a little nudge to make her get all the way over it. I got over it fast and grabbed her hand and we took off running again and didn't stop until we reached Jeb's barn.

Pa learned me how to drive before he went overseas. Ma said, at the time, that I was too little, but Pa went right ahead and learned me. I even drove Jeb's truck on the back roads a few times. That's how come I wasn't afraid of what I was planning to do.

The old truck was parked under a shelter to the side of the barn. I jumped up on the running board and jerked the door open, praying the key would be in it just like it always was. Sal climbed in on the other side and we closed the doors as quietly as we could. But I reckon no one could hear us anyway, what with the storm blowing all around us. The key was there, all right. I started up the truck and it hissed and sputtered and made us tremble in the seat. Then it died. Me and Sal looked at each other. I turned the key off and on again and pushed my boot down hard on the gas feed.

"What if it won't start?" Sal asked.

But it did start! This time it started right off with a pop and rattle and we spun off down Jeb's muddy dirt road that led to the back roads that wound up into the mountain.

Chapter
20

"I hear a wolf howling," Sal said, squinting her eyes and trying to see through the darkness and the rain that squiggled down the winder and all around the truck.

"That ain't no wolf. It's the wind in them old juniper trees," I told her, but I commenced to look all around too. On each side of us, as we rose higher and higher on the narrow roads, juniper and pine trees growed so thick it was as if they was locking the old truck in and they wasn't no way to go but up, higher and higher. I swallered and clutched the steering wheel a little tighter. I'd heard the same sound Sal had. It was a wolf, all right.

The old truck lumbered along, climbing the road at a crawl, dipping in and out of the rain-swollen ruts, like it was accustomed to such a heavy chore. And I reckon it was, seeing as how coming into the mountain was about all Jeb used the truck for. He hauled timber for firewood on the flat bed.

"Arney, what if Miz Simpson don't want to let Amelia come back with us?" Sal asked.

140

"Don't matter," I told her, gripping the steering wheel harder. "We got to bring her home with us."

We rose slower with the truck wheezing and rattling like some old man caught in a asthma attack.

"I ain't never been to Reba Simpson's cabin," Sal said, like talking made her feel better.

"It ain't much further," I told her.

But it was. I'd been up there before and even in the bright sunlight and the dryness of summer, the place seemed to be lost up in the clouds, setting at the edge of the steep hill. We was silent then, listening to the rain pelting down like rocks on the roof of the old truck and against the winders. After a while, Sal said, "Miz Tinker says the next time Gussie gets a bad grade on his homework paper, she's going to stand him up in the corner and put a dunce cap on his head."

I chuckled. "That's pretty good." But I wasn't feeling like a chuckle or even talking about old Gussie. Just to keep that truck on the road took all of my attention.

"Miz Tinker says . . ."

"Dad-blame it, Sal, can't you keep your blabbering mouth shut? I don't give a durn *what* Miz Tinker says!" I gripped the steering wheel and leaned over it, peering out through the rain and spatters of mud that slid all over the winder.

Sal started whimpering. "I didn't want to come, Arney. I didn't want to come up to this old mountain!"

I bit my lip hard, mad at myself for flying off at Sal. "We got to get Amelia," I reminded her, just as the thunder boomed and lightning lit up the road and the trees on each side of us. Sal leaned her head over and commenced to cry.

141

"Why . . . why don't you make up one of your songs, Sal? I sure would like to hear one of your songs," I said, wishing she'd stop crying and mad as the devil at myself for snapping at her.

Sal sniffed and rubbed at her eyes and sat up straight. We was still and quiet for a time and then she started to sing slowly. Her voice was low and I could hardly hear her above the sound of the truck chugging along.

"I . . . I'm gonna . . . turn myself around . . . and around . . . and if I fall to the ground . . . ground . . . ground . . ." she sang.

"That's a good one," I told her, feeling a little better.

"Then I'm gonna pick myself up . . . dust myself off . . . off . . . off . . ." Sal sang on, getting a little louder.

"I sure do like that one," I told her. But the truth was, in that moment, I would of liked anything she wanted to sing.

"I'm gonna turn myself around AND AROUND AND IF I FALL TO THE GROUND . . . GROUND . . . GROUND . . ." Sal sang out louder, her voice filling up the truck and taking the sound of the rain away.

I made a slow, cautious turn on the steep road and looked over to the side. There wasn't no trees anymore. They wasn't nothing but a swift drop off down into a deep canyon for anyone who missed the turn. I gripped the steering wheel even harder. If I wasn't careful and didn't watch the light from the headlights on the road, the truck could go tumbling over before I could blink an eye.

"I'M GONNA TURN MYSELF AROUND . . ." I joined in with Sal, yelling out so loud my ears started to ring. "AROUND AND AROUND AND AROUND . . ." we sang on like we was both trying to chase our fear away.

142

After a while we come to another turn in the road and started to climb again. I switched the old truck into gear and felt it jerk and pull back, then it commenced to slowly go forward, chugging and snorting up through the darkness all around us. I looked to the side of the road again but, this time, I couldn't even see over the edge. All I could see was deep blackness that made a chill run all through me.

"AND AROUND AND AROUND AND AROUND . . ." We sang until I felt like I was getting dizzy. But I knowed it was keeping Sal occupied and further away from crying.

"Look!" Sal said suddenly and she leaned forward, pointing a finger. Up ahead, caught in the headlights was an old cabin that seemed to teeter on the brink of all that blackness. It sat almost at the edge of the hill, looking like the only thing that kept it from falling over the side was the trees that growed near it. There was a light in the winders and I sighed with relief. It was Reba Simpson's cabin.

I drove ahead a little ways more and turned into the wide yard where the cabin sat and stopped the truck. Me and Sal looked all around. It was hard to make out anything in the darkness, but we could see a porch on the cabin and another building across the yard with what looked like a huge stack of firewood leaning against it.

"Let's make a run for the porch!" I told Sal.

We got out of the truck as fast as we could and dashed through the slick mud and pouring rain and up the steps of the porch. I banged on the door with my fist and shouted. "Miz Amelia! Miz Amelia Martin! You in there?"

143

It wasn't a minute or two and the door was whipped open and Amelia stood there with a surprised look on her face. But there was happiness there too. Like she was glad to see someone.

"Arnold! Sally! What are you two doing here?" she cried, and she reached out her arms to us. "My goodness, what a surprise! Who did you come with?" She looked around us, out on the porch, but she could see we was alone and only the darkness and the rain splashed onto the porch.

"We come to get you, Miz Amelia, and take you home to our house," Sal said soon as Amelia stopped hugging her.

"You two young'uns come to get me?" Amelia asked, and her dark eyes got big and wide. She looked from Sal to me and back again. "I can't believe it! How did you get up here?"

Me and Sal exchanged a look. "Well, you see . . ." I glanced at Sal again. She was fidgiting. "We . . . we borried Jeb Worth's truck and, well . . . Ma was going to come, but Miz Crimp was due to have her baby and she had to go tend to her."

"Well, for goodness sake," Amelia exclaimed. "Come over close to the fire and take off them wet coats." She closed the door and we follered her to the feeble looking fire. It was cold in the cabin and I could tell Amelia had set the fire herself and hadn't done a very good job of it. There was wood in a box next to the hearth and I set about to build up the fire.

I glanced around while I worked at the fire. There sure wasn't nothing homey ner inviting about the place. It was just an old cabin with splintery walls and floors and a few

144

old dusty-looking pictures hanging around. The furniture was old and rustic and even the tabletops didn't have doilies on them the way Ma's tables did.

"I can't believe that you two come all the way up here and in this storm," Amelia said as she watched me put the logs into the fireplace.

"Ma wants you to come and live with us until your husband comes home," Sal said, taking off her coat and shaking the rain off of it.

Amelia told her to hang her coat on a hook near the door and when Sal went to do it, Amelia sat down in a hard-backed chair beside the fireplace and pulled her shawl closer around her shoulders.

"Where is Miz Simpson?" I asked.

"She went down to Weedpatch a few days ago and I reckon, with the storm and all, she decided to stay at Lessie Fay's Boarding House. I expect her back at any time. When I first heard you knock on the door I thought it was her," Amelia answered and suddenly a pained look overtook her face and she touched her belly.

"Are you all right, Miz Amelia?" Sal asked, jumping to her side.

"I've had a few pains for the past hour," Amelia said in a voice that matched the look on her face.

"Maybe you ought to go to bed," Sal suggested.

"No . . . I'll be fine . . . Oh!" Amelia cried, and throwed her head back. The look on her face now was pure agony. I stood up with my heart pounding. Sal looked at me and her eyes was all full of fear. "I . . . I reckon you're right, Sally," she went on like she couldn't hardly get the words out.

Me and Sal hurried to get on each side of her and help

her into the bedroom. Her shawl fell to the floor as we walked, me and Sal holding on to her arms, and I stared at her belly. I didn't see how it could get much bigger. I'd never seen no woman in a family way with a belly so big. But I reckoned, if they *was* twins in there like Ma suspected, they would need all that room.

We walked slowly and with each step, Amelia's face looked struck with a new pain. Finally, in the bedroom, which was only a big bed with an old dresser and a few odds and ends of furniture on the bare floor, we helped Amelia lay down.

"Thank you," Amelia said as her body sunk down into the mattress and her head laid against the piller. She sighed like she was exhausted.

Sal took a quilt from the foot of the bed, covered Amelia with it, and give me another fearful look. I commenced to get an uneasy feeling that Amelia might be getting ready to have her baby.

"Anyone else live around here close, Miz Amelia?" I asked, feeling helpless along with uneasy.

"Only Benny Pool's daddy. His place is a few miles down the road," Amelia answered, frowning up at me from the bed. That pained look hadn't left her face. Benny Pool's daddy was an old hermit who hadn't stuck his head out his door since Benny died in the war.

"Arney can go and get him, if you want him to," Sal said like she was afraid for us to be alone with Amelia, and her in so much pain.

"I don't expect that will be necessary, Sally. Miz Simpson ought to be back any time now and she'll know just what to do, if I need her," Amelia answered, and I noticed her fingers begin to twitch against her huge belly. "Any-

146

way, I've been feeling pretty good up to now. I'm sure I'm just a little tired, is all."

"I better go and stoke up the fire. It feels chilly in here," I said, and as I walked out of the bedroom, I saw Amelia's fingers grab at the quilt that lay over her and squeeze it tight in her hand. That uneasy feeling hit me full force then.

"Can I get some hot tea for you, Miz Amelia?" I heard Sal ask.

"That would be nice, Sally, honey. The kettle is on the stove in the kitchen," Amelia said, and her voice sounded all wore out.

Sal come and stood in the doorway of the front room staring at me as I stoked up the fire and got it to blazing good. The cabin was so old and drafty it creaked and snapped every time a gust of wind hit it. I couldn't understand how Reba Simpson would want to live in such a lonely, cold place, much less bring Amelia up there to it. But Reba Simpson wasn't like most women. She was more like the cabin, rough and rustic.

"Arney," Sal said behind me, and I looked around. "I'm afraid."

"Ain't nothing to be afraid of, Sal," I said, turning back to the fire. "You heard what Amelia said. It ain't time for her baby to come. Besides, this ain't as bad as being out on the road in Jeb's old truck."

As I spoke, the wild and lonely sound of a wolf come calling out through the wind. I turned and give Sal another look. "Shoot," I said with a shrug, "that ain't nothing but the wind." I stood up and took off my coat and went to hang it on the hook next to Sal's coat.

"It ain't neither, Arney, and you know it!" Sal said, and

I shot a look at her. Her face showed all the fear and dread she had inside.

I went back to the fireplace, kneeled down and, before I could think of what to say, Amelia let out a low moan that sent a chill up my back.

"Edward! . . . Edward!" she cried out suddenly, and I wished with all my heart that her husband was there with her in that old cabin on that cold, wet mountain, instead of me and Sal.

Chapter
21

I stoked harder and harder at the fire, trying to keep a good blaze going, but every time it got going good, a puff of wind would blow down through the chimley and almost put it out. Amelia kept calling and calling for her husband until it near about drove me out of that cabin. But I couldn't of opened the door to the outside even if I'd wanted to. The wind was blowing so hard, I reckoned that door was jammed tighter than a cork in a jug. I wouldn't of wanted to leave, anyway. Not with that old wolf howling every so often.

I sure wished I was back home with Buck and Bill laying on the floor beside me, and Gobble flying around outside and the chickens clucking around under the house and Ma making coffee and Granny rocking and singing. Gobble . . .

Just remembering poor old Gobble made me start to hating old man Hooker all over again. This was his fault too. If it hadn't been for him, Amelia, his own blood daughter, wouldn't be in the fix she was in.

Sal had gone in the bedroom to be with Amelia, but

from the sound of it, she couldn't quiet her down. Poor Sal, I thought, she didn't even want to come and now here she was in a storm on top of Brushy Mountain with wolves howling and Amelia Martin carrying on something fierce.

But after a little, Amelia quieted down and Sal was back in the doorway asking, "*Where is* Miz Simpson, Arney? Why don't she come?"

"She'll be here, Sal. Amelia said she'd be here any time." I wished I could believe my own words, but deep inside me I had a sinking feeling that made me question if Reba Simpson might not come at all!

Sal left the doorway and I went to jabbing at the fire again and watching the tiny red and yeller sparks fly up from the flame. Seemed like I was stoking at that fire more than it needed it, just to keep myself busy and out of that bedroom where Amelia laid.

After some little time, I got the feeling Sal was watching me. She didn't have to say a word. It seemed like the wind made a person know a lot they wouldn't of otherwise knowed. I turned my head and seen her in the doorway again. I had to catch my breath! I could see the flicker of the firelight in the sweat that shined on her face and I could see her eyes looking big and black with torment. She kept twisting her hands round and round like she was in a nervous flurry.

"What's wrong, Sal?" I asked, half afraid of what she would answer.

"Why ain't Reba Simpson here?" she cried out. "Why ain't she come?"

I turned back to the fireplace and jabbed hard at the

logs. One split in, sent out a hissing noise, a hundred sparks exploding all around it, then rose and shot up the flue. "She'll be here, Sal," I said as calmly as I could. *"Don't worry!"* Inside me, my belly lurched and chugged with a sick feeling. *Where was* Reba Simpson, anyway? *Why* wasn't she here like she was supposed to be?

All at once Amelia's cries shot across the cabin and my blood froze. Me and Sal stared at each other for a split second, then she said in a low, trembling voice, "You'd better come and help me, Arney."

My heart commenced to pound and whipped my blood to flowing again.

"I think . . . I think Amelia's baby is getting ready to be born."

"What?" My yell was louder than Amelia's cries.

"That baby is getting ready to be born and you got to help me, Arney."

Birth a baby! Babies just come, didn't they? How come you had to help them, anyway? I shook my head hard, back and forth. "No," I said, firm as I could. "You seen Ma do what she had to do many times. You know what to do, Sal. You don't need me."

"You *got* to help, Arney! Ain't no one else here to help me and I can't do it by myself! All I ever done when I was with Ma was mind the young'uns and pat sweat off the faces of the women and make tea and such!"

"It's different now, Sal. You're the one that's got to do what Ma always done," I told her as I watched a terrified darkness flood over her face.

Sal's lips commenced to tremble and tears sped out of her eyes. They made a stream down through the flicker of

151

firelight that shone on her sweaty cheeks. "Ain't no way I can do it alone," she said, and her whole body seemed to sag like she'd come to the end of a long, long walk and she was too tired to take another step. I stood up and went to her and much as I hated saying it, I told her I would help her. Her face brightened and she took a deep breath and said, "We got to get a knife, Arney."

"What?"

"They is a knife in the kitchen in a drawer. You get the knife and hold it over the fire on the stove for a few minutes."

"Why?"

"To make it sterile. Ma says the knife has to be sterile to cut the baby's cord."

"*Cord!*" What was all this about, anyway! Sterile knives and cords!

"That's how the baby gets fed till it's born. The cord has to be cut away from the mother," Sal went on, even though I was looking so dumbfounded, she might ought to have laughed.

At the sound of Amelia crying out, we took off into the kitchen, me ahead of Sal and her right at my heels. While I found the knife and turned on the stove to hold the blade over the fire, Sal went to the sink and commenced pumping water to wash her hands so's they'd be good and clean when she helped Amelia. After just a minute, the blade was red hot. Sal dried her hands on a clean towel from a drawer and handed me one to lay the knife on, then together we raced from the kitchen and into the bedroom.

My innerds was so twisted around inside me by then

that they felt like they was being knotted into a rope. Soon as we got into the room, Amelia let out another loud holler. I started to tremble and couldn't stop. All I wanted to do was turn tail and run! But I knowed I couldn't leave Sal alone with what she had to do.

Amelia's head snapped back and forth on the piller. Her eyes was closed and sweat glittered across her face the same as it did on Sal's. Her hands clutched the metal bars of the bedstead behind her, making her knuckles look all white and bony. I swallered again and again, trying to keep my mouth from going dry, but it just got dryer and dryer.

"Get up on the bed, Arney! Get behind Amelia and grab her hands and let her hang on to you," Sal told me.

"No!" I blasted, and I glared at Sal.

"Amelia needs the feel of human hands! Not them metal bars!" Sal almost sobbed.

I studied Sal in a quick, new way. She sounded like Ma, telling me what to do, knowing what was the best way and never being wrong about it. But the idea of getting on that bed didn't set right with me.

"I *can't* do that!" I cried out as I handed her the towel with the knife on it. My whole body was shaking.

"You got to!" Sal cried back, pleading at me with her voice and her eyes. She laid the towel on the edge of the bed and dropped her head into her hands and started crying so hard her shoulders shook. "Ma . . . Ma . . . !" she moaned over and over.

I rushed to her and put my arms around her, feeling her shake against me. "D-don't cry, Sal! Please don't cry! I'll . . . I'll do it!" I patted her shoulder, trying to reassure her,

153

but all the while I was praying the cabin door would fly open and Reba Simpson would walk through it.

Sal lifted her head, took a deep breath and moved toward Amelia. I hurried to get up on the bed behind Amelia and started twisting her fingers away from the bars of the bedstead. When I finally got her hands into mine, her long fingernails cut deep into my palms. I wanted to cry out in pain, but I reckoned there was already enough crying going on in that room, so I bit into my lip and held back as best I could. With Amelia still hanging on, I got my balance on the bed and stood up. She tossed her head and continued to moan for her husband.

Sal lifted the blanket away from Amelia and commenced to minister to her like she seen Ma do when she went with her to birth babies. I could tell from the expression on her face she was praying this was all a dream and that she'd wake soon and be at home, in her room, and Ma would be there. Poor Sal. If I hadn't begged her to come! But she was working at helping that baby to come. I studied her hard. The sweat was still on her face and her hair hung in wet curls around her face. I looked away, biting into my lip as hard as Amelia's fingernails was biting into my hands and stared across the room. I could hear the swish, swish noise of the tree branches scraping against the roof, the whistling sound the wind made traveling through the cracks in the walls and the creaking and snapping the cabin made when the wind hit it hard. It seemed like I could feel the walls sway and the bed move like the floor had tilted and, way off in the wind and thunder, was the lonesome howl of that wolf.

Where was Reba Simpson? I wondered until my mind felt raw from it. I commenced to feel wore out too, like hours was passing. My back ached and my hands was sore and my feet trembled on the bed. I wanted to shout when suddenly Amelia's cries exploded like the loud clapping thunder and Sal shrieked, "It's here, Arney! The baby is here! But . . . but it's stuck! Arnie, it ain't coming right!"

"You got to help it, Sal," I yelled. Sal looked up at me with the face of a girl dumbfounded by fear. "Sal!" I yelled again.

"It's breech, Arney!" Sal shouted as fierce as the storm clamoring around the cabin and a chill ran up and down my back and all inside me. I knowed what "breech" meant. I'd heard Gussie tell how his little brother come into the world feet first and how he couldn't git enough air that way. Ma called it a "breech birth."

Please come *now*, Miz Simpson . . . *please*! I prayed. But she didn't come and somehow Sal got control of herself and commenced working with the baby. "Come on, baby," she kept saying real low, "come on." I looked away, biting my lips hard, trying to think of other things, but I couldn't. I was too aware of how Sal was trying to help the little baby.

It seemed like long hours of time passed again before she got the baby out and cut and tied the cord. But she soon exploded with a new horror.

"I got the baby, Arney . . . but it ain't moving. Arney! Arney! The baby won't move!"

"Pick it up and spank it, Sal!" I screeched in a voice that burned my throat. My body was shaking more than ever now and my feet was doing a crazy, nervous dance on the mattress. "Do it!" I screeched again.

Sal looked up at me as though I'd brought her out of a

155

stupor. Then she bent and scooped the baby up in her two hands like she'd of ruther died than to do it, and she give the baby a couple of easy spats. But no sound come from the baby. It was limp in Sal's arms.

"It's dead!" Sal whimpered, looking up at me with wild eyes. "Arney! It's dead!"

But they was no time for grievin ner nothing, because Sal no more than got them words out when Amelia cried out and gripped my hands even harder. I winced from the pain of it. But my hands was near about numb now from her fingernails gouging into them.

"It's . . . it's *another* one! Arney! They is another baby coming!" Sal cried like she couldn't believe what she was seeing.

Ma had been right! Amelia *was* carrying twins! I stared hard at the blanket that covered Amelia and all the secrets of birth. Then Sal made a quick move and my eyes was drawn back to her. She laid the little dead baby on the bed and covered it with Amelia's shawl, then moved back toward her.

For a moment Sal looked helpless. Then her face went serious, and she commenced to go right to work again. "It's here," Sal said after a few minutes had passed. This time Sal picked the baby up as soon as it come from Amelia and spatted its bottom like she knowed just what she was doing. A small, gurgly little cry entered the room. I stared down at the new baby. It was shiny and wet looking. My eyes met Sal's and we started to cry. Then we commenced to laugh for some strange, crazy reason. But I reckon the crying was for the little dead baby and the laughing was for the alive one. After a little while, we stopped carrying on and looked down at the other baby wrapped in the shawl. How was we going to tell Amelia, I wondered.

I looked down into Amelia's face. She was quiet now with her eyes tightly closed and her lips still pressed together. Sweat covered her face and the creases in her forehead. Somehow she had fallen asleep. I reckoned she was plumb wore out. All at once I realized that she wasn't hanging on to my hands. *I* was hanging on to hers! I let them go gently and laid her arms across her breast and got down off the bed. Then I went and looked at the little dead baby with its eyes forever closed to the world and its brain not able to think, and I understood for the first time what death was.

It was stillness and silence and never knowing to laugh or cry, and never seeing the trees and flowers and the sky filled with clouds, or hearing the wind or the birds, and never being touched and held and hugged or looking into your own Mama's eyes. It was a spirit that wasn't strong enough to survive, that wasn't strong enough to leave the darkness and come into the light.

I moved away from the bed and went to look at the other baby. Sal had cut the cord and tied it just like she'd done it a hundred times before. Now she was wrapping the baby in an old afghan she'd pulled off a chair near the bed. I studied the little alive baby, its small head moving and its little fingers trying to find its mouth and at its eyes opening and closing and the tiny little whimpering it made.

"They is both boys, Arney," Sal said in a tired voice as she laid the new baby on the bed next to Amelia.

157

"Twin boys," I said in awe, and Sal nodded her head.

Old man Hooker come into my mind then. I tried not to think about him, but the little boys, the dead one and the live one, was his own gran'sons. Well, I reckoned the dead one was just as well off for the old man was sure to hate the alive one just as much as he hated everyone else. All at once it come into my mind how I wanted old man Hooker dead and now, a part of him was dead! Could all my mean thoughts have caused the baby to die? I stared at the still face of the baby, feeling ashamed with guilt and praying inside that what I'd wished on old man Hooker hadn't come true for his little gran'baby.

The baby commenced to whimper. Sal picked him up and held him close in her arms. "When Amelia wakes up she'll be needing some hot tea to revive her and something to eat."

"I'll find something," I said, and I went to the door, but I stopped and looked back at the dead baby on the bed next to his mother. "Sal, what are we going to do about . . ."

Sal's eyes went to the dead twin. Then she looked at me. "We'll have . . . have to tell Amelia when she wakes up," she said in a pain-filled whisper.

I walked out of the room and went to the kitchen. At the sink I pumped water into the kettle for Amelia's tea and set it on the stove. Then I sat down at the table and listened to the sounds the cabin made. But now there was a new sound. A baby crying.

When I'd finished fixing the tea and poured it in a cup, I found some bread and honey on a shelf. I poured the honey on a slab of bread and put it on a plate and carried it and the cup of tea into the bedroom. Soon as I walked through the door, I seen that Sal had wrapped the dead baby in a piller case and laid him on a piller in a chair beside the bed. She had left the other baby next to Amelia on the bed. On the other side of the bed, Sal was setting in a rocking chair with her eyes closed. Amelia was still sleeping.

I went up to Sal. "Here, Sal," I said, offering her the cup of tea. "I can make more for Amelia."

Sal opened her eyes and took the cup. She sipped at the tea like she hadn't had anything to drink in a week. I set the plate with the bread on it on the table next to the bed and went to set down on the floor. I leaned against the wall and could feel it snap and sway next to my back when the wind hit it hard.

Off in the distance, over the wind, that wolf commenced to howl and the sound of thunder made the cabin vibrate while lightning flashed and cracked and lit up the whole room. In the bed Amelia stirred and opened her eyes.

Chapter

22

Amelia looked around the room with her eyes as big as a cat's eyes, like she wasn't sure where she was. Her face was all pale and drawn, like she'd been working at some hard job all night long. Fact of the matter is, I reckon having a baby, and most especially *two* babies, is a hard job. Sal got up and went over to the bed.

"You got a little baby boy, Miz Amelia," she said softly.

Amelia looked just like it dawned on her where she was and what had happened. She looked around and seen the baby laying beside her and smiled. "Oh . . . it's my baby . . ." she whispered, and her face brightened. She leaned over and reached for the little feller and pulled him into her arms. "Oh . . . so sweet . . ." she whispered to the baby and she put a tiny kiss on his forehead. Then she looked up at Sal. "Thank you for . . . for h-helping me, Sally . . . I'm . . . I'm grateful you was here." There was tiredness in her words and on her face.

"Arney helped too," Sal spoke up, and Amelia's eyes moved around the room until she seen me setting against the wall.

"I'm grateful to you too, Arnold," she said, and she smiled at me. "But . . . I remember . . . where is my other baby? They was two." A heavy frown took over where her smile had been.

Me and Sal exchanged a look. "Well . . ."

I got up and went to the bed. Sal needed help in telling Amelia about the other baby. It looked like she never would get the words out. I was plenty brave thinking I could explain everything until I got to the bed. Then my voice went away and all I could do was stare at Amelia just like Sal was doing. Amelia looked from me to Sal with them catlike eyes snapping out in question.

"Something is wrong, ain't it. I know it is. I can tell," Amelia said suspiciously. Her eyes moved back and forth across me and Sal.

"Y-yes, ma'am," Sal managed to mutter, and she looked down with her face crumbling.

"What is it? Where is my other baby?" Amelia's voice rose.

Sal stepped away from the bed, letting Amelia see the chair where the dead baby laid. Amelia made a heavy noise way down deep in her throat and raised up to stare at the lifeless baby on the piller. All at once she tried to get out of the bed, but holding the baby, she couldn't. She clutched him tighter in her arms and gasped like she would die.

"He's . . . he's dead, Miz Amelia." I stammered the words out with a deep heaviness in my heart.

"No . . . no . . . no . . ." she cried, raising up even higher and glaring at the dead baby.

"He . . . it couldn't be helped," Sal said in a low

161

whimper. "He . . . he come first and he was . . . was 'breech' and . . ."

"Give him to me!" Amelia demanded, and she sank back against the piller and opened her arms to receive the baby.

Sal leaned over and picked the baby up as gently as she could and laid him in the crook of Amelia's arm just like she was holding the other baby. When he was settled there, Amelia kissed him and tears trickled from her eyes. I stared at the dead baby's face. His eyes was shut tight and he had a placid look, like he was only sleeping and, any minute, you could touch him and he'd open his eyes. He looked exactly like the other baby. There wasn't no difference that I could see. They both had small knots of light hair on their heads and, I reckon, looked like their daddy.

Me and Sal stood beside the bed quietly watching Amelia holding both babies with tears streaming down her face. I wished that Sal could make up one of her songs and sing it. I wished she could sing it to the top of her lungs, *anything* to change the dark feeling in that room.

A sudden strong gust of wind hit the walls of the cabin and seemed to make it sway in one direction, to groan, like they was going to collapse. I never heard such a wind as howled and clamored around that cabin. Outside there was the sound of things flying against the cabin, of tree branches slapping at the walls. Amelia clutched hard at the babies and held them close until the cabin settled and the wind died down. The baby whimpered and moved, waking up.

"Arnold," Amelia said in a voice that was calm and direct, like she'd done spent her emotion, "take a drawer out of the dresser there and empty out what is in it. Sally, you get a clean towel out of the kitchen and line the drawer with it."

Me and Sal moved quick to do what Amelia told us to do. I was glad to be able to do something. It was better than just standing there next to the bed and watching Amelia's pain. I pulled out the top drawer of the dresser and took out the clothes that was in it. They was old shirts and things that looked like they'd belonged to Reba Simpson's dead husband. I reckoned she got plenty use out of them, though, seeing as how that's all she ever wore. No one never did see her in a dress after her husband died. She sure was a curiosity everywhere she went.

I carried the drawer to the chair beside the bed and set it down. Sal come back from the kitchen with a towel and laid it in the bottom of the drawer. When she was finished, she looked up at Amelia with a deep sadness in her face.

"Now come and pick up the baby, Sally, and lay him in the drawer gently as you can. Cover his head with the pillercase he's wrapped in. Then the both of you pick up the drawer and set it on top of the dresser," Amelia directed us like she didn't feel no emotion at all now. But deep down inside her I knowed she did. She let Sal take the baby out of her arms and watched as she laid him in the drawer as soft and as gentle as a whisper. Then Sal pulled the piller case up over his head, and we each took an end of the drawer and carried it over to the dresser and set it on top. I watched Sal's face. Her chin was quivering and tears was in her eyes. I looked down at the piller case and bit hard into my lip to keep from letting go with my feelings. It was hard to think of the little baby being under that piller case.

163

When we was finished and went back to the bed, Amelia was nursing the other baby with his face pressed up against her breast. "Thank you, children," she said in a tired voice. "Thank you for everything," she said again, and laid her head back against the piller and shut her eyes. Me and Sal went to set down, Sal in the rocking chair and me on the floor against the wall.

I leaned back and closed my eyes. Death sure did make a person feel worn out, all right. It made you feel like your whole insides was drained right out of you. I reckon I fell asleep thinking on that because, the next thing I knowed, I could hear Sal's voice way, way off in the distance, like it was surrounded by some kind of mist, singing her made-up song about Brushy Mountain.

"Brushy Mountain . . . Brushy Mountain . . . what secret do you knoooowww . . ." Then Sal's voice faded away and another voice come and took its place. It sounded like a man's voice, only it was *my* voice and I was all growed up and looking tall and straight, just like Pa. The growed-up me was saying strange things like, "The thing about life, Arney, is there is holding on and there is letting go."

"You mean, letting go, like we had to do when Pa died?" I asked like I was young again and remembering all the pain of that time.

"Yes, Arnold Burdette. But there is something even more important than that."

"What?" I demanded to know, laying there staring at that misty stranger who was the growed-up me.

"There is going on."

"Going on? Like Ma done when she learned Pa wasn't

164

coming back from the war?" I asked, like I just understood what was being said to me.

"Yes, Arney. Going on just like Ma done. Goooing oooooon . . . Goooing oooon . . . !" The voice sounded like it was getting further and further away and finally I couldn't hear it no more.

"Come back!" I shouted. "Come back here!" I woke up suddenly, feeling the wind hit the cabin again and the wall sway behind my back. Who am I? I wondered. Am I that growed-up man who said all them strange things? Or am I me, Arney Burdette, just like I was yesterday and the day before? I rubbed my eyes and looked over at Sal, setting limply in the rocking chair and just opening her eyes. I reckoned then that I was still me. And I was glad.

Sal looked all around the room like she'd forgot everything that had happened, but when her eyes lit on Amelia and the baby, I could tell she remembered everything. Amelia and the baby was both sleeping. I stood up, feeling weak and unsteady, and went to the table next to the bed and drunk down the tea Sal had left in the bottom of the cup and picked up the slab of bread and et it. Sal got up and whispered, "Let's go to the kitchen, Arney." I follered her, carrying the empty plate and cup and munching on the bread.

In the kitchen Sal warmed water in the kettle for the tea and we sat down at the table with a round, empty butter dish in the middle of it. I took the lid and commenced to fiddle with it.

"What are we going to do, Arney?" Sal asked through the stillness that wasn't still at all, but alive with all the sounds the wind made. But it was still too, with the feel and aloneness of death.

I thought of my dream and shivered. Was the grown-up me trying to tell me a person had to go on with life, no matter if there was death in it? I had to shiver again, just to think about it. Then it come to me! Everything the growed-up me meant! All them words, "letting go," and "holding on"! They all meant the same thing! *Surviving! That* was the secret of the mountain! Hadn't Sal and me survived the worst time in our whole lives with the birthing of Amelia's babies? Maybe *that* was the secret of Sal's song and the secret of Brushy Mountain, without Sal even knowing it.

"What are we going to do about Amelia and her babies?" Sal asked, and she got and brought the teapot and cups to the table and poured the tea for us. Then she sat down across from me. Her face was still dirty and tear streaked and her eyes looked hard, like she had been through an experience that made her change. She was still Sal, but she was different too.

"I reckon we'll have to leave that up to Amelia," I said, and I took a sip of the tea. "We can't take her down the mountain now. Not with them babies."

"Remember when Gobble was killed?" Sal asked.

"I won't never forget it."

"It was different from this."

"I know."

We sighed and took sips of our tea.

"I reckon Ma is worried sick about us."

I drunk all my tea down in three big gulps. I didn't notice if it scalded my tongue or not. I set the cup down and looked at Sal, right in her eyes. "I ain't sorry we come, Sal. No telling what would have happened if we hadn't come."

166

"I ain't sorry neither, Arney. I'm glad we could help Amelia."

Old man Hooker come slamming into my mind again. If the old fool had of acted right by his daughter and let her stay at his place, Ma could of birthed the babies. But wasn't no use to think about all that now. It was too late.

Sal started to say something else and stopped. Somewhere close by we heard the wolf howl again. We stared across the table at each other. The sound come again and it was as close as Buck and Bill sounded when they barked down by the barn.

Chapter
23

"I reckon I'd better stoke up the fire," I said, and Sal jumped up and follered me into the front room, so close at my heels, it felt like she was my shadder. I knowed she was afraid.

The fire was almost out. Suddenly I felt cold all the way through me. It was the first time I'd felt so cold since Amelia's babies come. I leaned down and picked up the stoker and jabbed at the logs. Sal stood close beside me. I got more wood out of the wood box next to the fireplace and put it in the fire. Sal stayed right next to me. I could hear her breathing almost as hard as the wind howling around the cabin. I turned and looked up at her and just as I did, the sound of the wolf come again, and close on it was the sound of another one. It wasn't a lonesome, faraway sound like it come from across a hill or down deep in a canyon. And it didn't sound like Buck and Bill down at the barn this time. The sound was closer. Like it was right next to the cabin.

I stood up and put my arm around Sal, needing to feel close to her maybe even more than she needed to feel close to me.

"Arney!" Sal cried.

"Them wolves can't get inside, Sal. Not unless they can turn a doorknob and open the door." I patted her back, trying to comfort her. "Long as they're outside and we're inside, we ain't got no worries. They can stay there and howl till the world turns a somersault." I said them brave words but inside I was as afraid as she was. "Go fix some hot tea for Amelia, Sal. And take her some bread. She'll probably be awful hungry when she wakes up," I said, and I took my arm away from her.

Sal give out with a deep sigh, turned around and hurried off to the kitchen. I stood there listening to her movements, waiting for her to leave the kitchen and go into the bedroom with Amelia and the babies. It was quiet outside now except for the wind. After what seemed like a long time, I heard Sal going into the bedroom. I rushed to the nearest winder and lifted the corner of the shade. Daylight had come. Where did all the night go? I wondered, as I peered out and let my eyes rove slowly across the yard, from one side to the other.

There was an old outhouse with the roof sagging to one side and the door hanging on its hinges and swinging back and forth in the wind. Pine needles and leaves and tumbleweeds covered the ground and scooted further and further across it as the wind blowed them. The branches of the trees swooped up and down and in all directions, blown by the wind. I looked into the sky. It was like the chalkboard in school after Miz Tinker wipes it clean and it looks totally gray. The far-off sound of thunder come from every corner of the sky, but the rain had almost stopped. Where was Reba Simpson? I wondered again. Why hadn't she come like Amelia said she would? Should I try to get Amelia and the babies down off the mountain? Was Ma looking for us? Had Jeb missed his truck? All these questions batted at my brain like hailstones.

I could hear Sal and Amelia talking softly in the bedroom and, every now and then, the baby whimpering. Then the voices stopped. I dropped the corner of the shade and turned around. Sal was coming up behind me.

"Amelia's awake," she said.

"What does she want us to do about the . . . the dead baby?" I asked.

"She ain't said. She just stares at the drawer on the dresser and don't say nothing."

"I reckon she's too filled with grief."

"I want to go home, Arney!" Sal cried suddenly. "I want to go home and see Ma and eat and change my clothes and lay down in my bed!"

Tears commenced running down her cheeks through the smudges of sweat and dirt. "Remember when you sung that song at Daphne Hazelton's birthday party? I sure would like to hear it again," I told her.

"I can't remember what I sung!" Sal blasted, looking filled with anger that I'd asked for a song at such a time.

"Well . . . make up another one. You always been able to do that." I knowed if Sal could sing, it would calm her nerves and make her feel better. Fact of the matter, I knowed it would make me feel better.

Before Sal made up her mind to sing or not, we heard Amelia calling out weakly through the walls to us. We took off like a shot to the bedroom. Amelia was staring at the drawer on top of the dresser where the dead baby laid. Her face looked tired and sad and all the prettiness seemed

170

took right out of it. We went up to the bed and Amelia's eyes moved from the dresser to us.

"I've been thinking that a child ought to have a name to be remembered by. And since the two of you helped with the birthing, I'd be much obliged if you give my baby a name."

Me and Sal exchanged a look. "I can't think of no name, Miz Amelia," Sal said in a low voice.

"I can't neither," I said.

"Oh, but you must have a favorite name tucked away . . ."

I looked down at the floor, then up at Sal and over to Amelia in the bed. It sure was hard to think of names after all that had happened. But a name come into my mind and I said it. "I like the name of Morris."

Amelia smiled. "That was your daddy's name, wasn't it." I nodded. "Well, I'd be proud to have my little son named after your daddy. How does Edward Morris sound to you? Edward after my husband."

Me and Sal nodded our heads and tried to smile.

"What are you going to name the other baby?" I asked.

"Tice will be one of his names," Amelia answered, and me and Sal shot a quick look at each other.

Tice! How could she even want to give her baby old man Hooker's name? I wondered with pure disgust. It was because of him that she had come up to the mountain in the first place!

"Do you want us to raise the shade? It's daylight now," Sal said like she was trying to change the subject.

Amelia sighed. "No, not just yet. Would you bring Edward Morris to me now?" she asked, and we follered her

171

eyes to the drawer across the room on the dresser. "I want to kiss him goodbye."

Me and Sal went to the dresser and lifted the drawer down as gently as we could, with Sal on one end of it and me on the other. Then we carried it to the bed and Amelia leaned over as best she could and pulled the piller case away from the baby's face and kissed him on his forehead. I waited for the baby to open his eyes. He looked so alive, I almost forgot that he was dead.

"First Pa, then Gobble. Now little Edward Morris," Sal said in a low, pained whisper close to my ear.

"Yeah," I whispered back. "Seems like we've seen too much death lately. And I'm getting durned tired of it too!" I had to sniff hard to pull back the tears I wanted to cry.

Amelia laid back against her piller and pulled the other baby close in her arms. Then she closed her eyes. "You can take him back to the dresser now," she said in a faint voice.

Sal covered the baby's face with the piller case and we picked up the drawer and carried it back to the dresser and set it on top. Then we left Amelia with her eyes closed, hugging the other baby to her, and went out of the room.

In the front room, Sal sat down in the chair next to the fireplace and looked across the room like she was thinking real hard. Pretty soon she shut her eyes and commenced to hum a little tune. I went over and laid down on the bare floor in front of the fire, wishing old Buck and Bill was there with me. Sal stopped humming and started in to singing softly and so sweetly it near about made me forget about the mountain and the wolves and Amelia's little dead baby.

172

"Rest your weary hearrrrt upon the clouuuuds . . .
And let them carrrry your troubles awaaaaay . . ."

I turned over on my belly and stretched my arms up to lay my head on them and closed my eyes, listening to Sal's song. Her voice rose and fell, trembling over her made-up words. I reckon I fell asleep because what happened next was, I opened my eyes to the sound of wolves calling out way, way off in the distance somewhere. I sat up. No sound come from the yard. I looked over at Sal. She was asleep in the chair with her head resting on her shoulders. A little fluttery snore fell from her lips.

I got up and went to look out the winder. The yard was still. Not even a leaf blowed. The wind had died away and the rain was just a soft spatter across the ground. The wolves was gone.

Chapter

24

W hile I stood at the winder I heard a distant SPUTTER-SPUTTER-POP-POP sound. Sal stirred in her chair and opened her eyes. "What's that noise, Arney?" she asked.

"I don't know," I answered, frowning out over the yard.

The SPUTTER-SPUTTER-POP-POP got closer and louder and Sal got up to come and stand at the winder next to me. We looked out toward the road and pretty soon we seen the ancient high-topped Peerless car that belonged to Reba Simpson turn into the yard. Steam was spewing out from the radiator like it was ready to explode.

"Reba Simpson!" Sal cried, and we beat it out the door, across the porch and down the steps into the yard just as the car pulled to a stop.

"What in the name of singed goose feathers are you two young'uns doing here? Your ma is beside herself with worry! Get out of the way! I've got to get that cap off before it blows off!" Reba Simpson yelled at us from the car winder and, not even waiting for an answer to her question, she jumped out of the car and rushed to yank the cap off the radiator. She had on canvas gloves, old gray, baggy pants and a brown jacket that was so big it near about swallered her. A blue bill cap perched on her head was turned to the side. Everyone knowed all them clothes she wore belonged to her dead husband. She could of passed for a man, if you didn't know her.

She got the cap off the radiator after twisting and jerking her hand away several times, and tossed it onto the ground at the same time she jumped away from the car. There was a loud SWISSSSHHHH noise as the steam exploded up out of the hole and met the cold air. Me and Sal jumped back.

"Hot damn!" Miz Simpson hollered as she watched the steam rise. After it settled a little, she turned to me and Sal and said, "What are you young'uns doing up here?" Before either one of us could answer, she pointed to the truck and said, "That truck over yonder belongs to Jeb Worth! I'd know it anywhere."

"Well . . ." I started, beginning to explain, but Miz Simpson whirled around and commenced marching to the cabin.

Sal called out before Miz Simpson reached the door. "Amelia had her babies!"

Miz Simpson stopped in her tracks with her hand on the doorknob, looked back at us and half whispered, "You don't tell me!" Her face was full of surprise.

"But one died," Sal told her.

Miz Simpson turned around then and touched her heart with her hand. "Merciful Jesus!"

"Two twin boys," Sal added, as we rushed up on the porch.

Miz Simpson shook her head and twisted her bill cap to make it straight. "I knowed I shouldn't of left her. I just knowed it. I should of come back sooner too. But the storm . . . well, it's too late to think about that now," she said with her eyes cast down to the top of her dead husband's old boots she wore.

"Me and Arney helped birth the babies," Sal said with a sad proudness in her voice.

Miz Simpson reached out and touched Sal's shoulder gently. "You *what!*" She shook her head again, like she couldn't believe it. "Well, thank the Lord you was here. But why on earth did you come up here?" Her face filled up with a questioning frown.

"Ma was going to come and get Amelia and take her home to live with us. But before she could get started, Roy Crimp showed up asking her to come quick to his place because his wife was ready to give birth," I said fast, with my words tumbling over each other.

"It didn't seem right for Ma to come up here in the storm after birthing Miz Crimp's baby," Sal joined in.

"Thinking of your ma," Miz Simpson said with a deep sigh and she reached up and twisted the bill on her cap to the side.

"Amelia's pa ain't about to let her live with him!" I said in a hard voice.

"That mean old snake! He ought to be hung!" Miz Simpson swung around then, turned the doorknob and walked through the door of the cabin. "Why, it's plumb warm in here," she said. "You must of set that fire, Arnold."

"He did, Miz Simpson," Sal said, and she give me a smile.

"And Sal made tea," I said, and give her a smile back.

"Well, from the looks of you two young'uns, you put a good five days' work into one. Your ma, worried as I know she is, ought to be mighty proud when she finds out what all has happened." Miz Simpson took off walking to the bedroom then and me and Sal sat down near the fireplace, me on the floor and Sal in the chair next to it.

I watched Sal look down at her overalls and run her fingers over the rough material. I thought about the dress she'd told me about and how she deserved to have it after all she'd went through.

Miz Simpson talked so loud that we could hear everything she said to Amelia in the bedroom. She told her she was going to put her and the baby in her car soon as she felt able to go down the mountain, but she was welcome to stay at the cabin as long as she liked, just like she'd told her before. What Amelia said was just a low mumble that we heard in between the baby whimpering.

It wasn't long before Miz Simpson come out of the bedroom carrying the baby and said, "He sure is a strong little feller. Too bad about the other little critter." She kissed the baby and looked at me and Sal. "You young'uns need a good cleaning up and some food in your bellies. I'll get some quilts and make pallets on the floor for you to rest on. You look mighty wore out, the both of you. I'll get some pertaters peeled and to boiling and . . ."

"I just want to go home, Miz Simpson," Sal spoke up.

Miz Simpson give Sal a tender look. "Well, I reckon you'd be too tired to eat a big meal anyway," she said. "I feel responsible to see you get home all right, but I can't leave poor Amelia . . . Arnold . . . ?" She give me a serious look. "You think you can get that flatbed truck back down the mountain?" I said I thought I could and she went on. "I'll fix up a little snack and you young'uns can be on your way before another storm comes up." She rested her chin on top of the baby's blanket where its head was and fixed me with another look. "I want you to be careful of the roads, Arnold. They're as slick as grease on a tin wash-tub."

"Yes, ma'am," I said. But I knowed them roads couldn't be no worse than when me and Sal drove up in them in the blackness of night.

Miz Simpson fixed us some sausage and we et it real quick with crackers. Soon as we finished, we cleaned up the kitchen for Miz Simpson, then we went in the bedroom to tell Amelia goodbye. But she was sleeping with the baby in her arms, so me and Sal tiptoed out without disturbing her. Before we left, I asked Miz Simpson about Edward Morris.

"He'll have a fine and proper burial when Amelia is ready. Don't you worry none about that," she told me.

Me and Sal couldn't wait to get into Jeb's truck. We took off down the mountain with the sun shining across the road and into the trees in the canyons on each side of us. Except for the dark corner of the sky, it was getting blue and clear. It sure felt good to be going home. I looked over at Sal. Her eyes was closed and her head was rolling gently against the back of the seat. She had a peaceful look on her face that I hadn't seen since coming up to Brushy Mountain. I looked back at the road and commenced to sing a little song. I couldn't sing as good as Sal ner make up songs the way she could, but the words just rolled right out of me.

"OH, BEAUTIFUL DAAAYYY . . . THE STORM HAS GONE AWAAAAY . . ."

Chapter

25

When we went clattering into the yard Granny was out to the side of the house feeding corn to the chickens. They was clucking and skittering around, digging their beaks into the ground for it. Granny looked up soon as she heard the truck and hurried through the chickens to us. They scattered, squawking and flying all around. Way down in the back field I could hear Buck and Bill barking. I knowed they was cutting a path up to the house to see what all the ruckus was about.

"Hey, Granny!" I called out the winder to her, and I give her a big grin. Sal got out of the truck almost before I could bring it to a stop and throwed her arms around Granny.

Granny hugged Sal back and Sal started crying and saying, "Oh . . . Granny . . . I'm soooo glad to see you!"

"Why, child, your face is dirty enough without you making it worse with all them tears," Granny said gently, and she patted Sal's back and rubbed at her hair. Then she looked over at me still in the truck and whipped out with, "Arnold Burdette, boy, where have you and this girl been?

Your mama has been walking a streak across the floor with worry and burning up the tires on that car of hers going up and down the roads looking for you! She's worried herself into a frenzy ever since she found you young'uns and that truck of Jeb's gone!"

Granny was almost into a frenzy herself when we told her where we'd been and what we had done. "Babies!" she cried like she was awestruck. "Glory be, your mama was right about Amelia going to have twins!"

While Sal was telling all the rest of what happened, Buck and Bill come running into the yard and charged right up to me wagging their tails and jumping up at me. They stood up on their hind legs and, one on each side of me, commenced to lick my cheeks. I hugged their necks till I near about choked them! I ain't never been so glad to see them hounds before ner since. A little while later me and Sal went in the house and Granny made us wash up and cooked up some greens and cornbread, just like Sal wanted.

"I want you young'uns clean and fed so's you can explain good and proper about things to your mama when she comes in. Why, the way you two look, you'd scare the tin cans right out of a billy goat!" Granny said when she brought the food to the table.

"Where is Ma, Granny?" I asked.

"Looking for you young'uns like she's been doing. She didn't get home from the Crimps' place till this morning. Lula's baby decided not to make an appearance until the sun rose," Granny answered. Then she give me a stern look over the top of her glasses and added, "You hadn't ought to of took that truck, Arnold."

181

"I'm going to take it back to Jeb's right now," I said, jumping up from my chair.

"Boy, stay and eat," Granny said. "They is plenty of time."

But I wouldn't stay. I took off in the truck and went directly to Jeb's place and when I drove up to the barn, I seen Jeb come striding out of his house with his thumbs stuck into the sides of his pants, heading straight for me. His jaw was set tight and there was a hardness in his eyes. I reckoned I was in for it. I got out of the truck and stood beside it, watching Jeb walking toward me. His expression never changed. I swallered and dug the toes of my brogans into the dirt. Jeb Worth sure could get a threat of a look on his face when he was of a mind to. I was near about to die when he finally reached me.

"Well, looks like you didn't run all the gas out of that truck," Jeb said when he got to me.

"No, sir. I reckon they might even be some left in it," I spoke right up. No need to hem and haw about it.

"That a fact," Jeb said, and he started walking around the truck, stopped and kicked the old tires, studied them for a minute and come back to stand in front of me. "Them tires don't look no more ragged than they did the last time I drove . . ."

"Jeb, I know you won't believe this," I cut right in, and Jeb come back with, "I might and I might not."

"Well," I went on nervously, and Jeb's expression didn't change. "You see, me and my sister, Sal, we took the truck and went up to the mountain to get Amelia because Ma was birthing Lula Crimp's baby, but Amelia, she had twin boy babies and . . ."

182

"You don't say!" Jeb said, and his stern face broke into a grin.

"Yes, sir, Sal birthed them, and one died . . ."

"No!" Jeb's face fell into sadness and his eyes grew dark.

"And then Miz Simpson, she finally come and . . ." I went on and on, filling in all the details and when I'd finished, Jeb slapped me on my back and said, "By God, if you ain't something! Saved old man's Hooker's life, then helped bring Amelia's babies into the world!" He scratched at his mustache a little, looked down, then up, then down again and up at me again. "Well, in a case like this, I reckon I'll just have to let it pass about you taking the truck," he said.

I sure was relieved about that. Jeb stuck out his hand and shook mine hard, like man to man. It was the first time I'd ever had my hand shook so hard.

"Come on up to the house. I'll give you a glass of cider before I drive you home," Jeb said, and he put his arm on my shoulder and we went up to the house. We drank the cider and he showed me all the pictures he had hanging on the walls of him when he was a boy and told me about some of the scrapes he got into. He even showed me a pair of real leather hand-tooled boots that had belonged to his gran'daddy and the stone head from a tommyhawk that he claimed was near about a hundred years old. I reckon we both let time get away from us. After he showed me them things he said, "Even though it wasn't the wisest thing for a boy to do, you took a real burden off your mama when you went up the mountain, Arnold. Knowing her, she would of gone up there in a hailstorm to help Amelia or anyone else."

183

"Yes, sir," I said, agreeing. I bit into my lip then because I was thinking.

"What is it, Arnold?" Jeb asked me.

"Well, sir, there's something I need to ask you. If my pa was here, I'd ask him."

Jeb smiled at me and took a drink of his cider. I could tell he was ready to listen.

"You see, I been wondering . . ." I started, and I went on and asked him if what I'd been thinking could be true. If me always wishing harm to old man Hooker could of, somehow, brought on the death of little Edward Morris.

Jeb set his glass down and put his hand on my shoulder. "I never put any store by such roundabout thoughts, Arnold," he said. "Folks thinking they can project their thoughts here and there and have them land on a gnat's ear just don't seem real to me. You couldn't of caused that little baby to die any more than you could of caused him to live. Such things as that are the works of the Lord, not humans."

I sighed deeply with my relief. Just to hear Jeb say them things made me feel lots better.

"Now, you get them notions out of your mind, Arnold Burdette," he went on, and he shook my shoulder real hard, like he meant business.

"Yes, sir," I said.

"Hey, we'd better get you home! Your mama will start thinking you've been kidnapped!" Jeb said all of a sudden.

Jeb drove me home right then and let me off on the road. Up at the house, I could see Ma's car and her standing in the doorway. I walked toward the house slow and easy and, when I got to it, Ma opened the door all the way and pulled me into her arms. "I ain't never been as worried in my life!" she cried.

"Did Sal tell you everything?" I asked.

"Yes," Ma answered, letting me go. "And I can hardly believe it."

"Are you mad at me, Ma?"

"I was at first. Mad and worried. But I'm glad now. Glad you and Sally are all right and that you could be there to help Amelia in her time of need." They was a little tear sparkling in the corner of Ma's eye. She pulled me back to her and give me another hug. "Now, you go on in the house. If you're as wore out as Sally, you'll be wanting nothing more than to crawl right into bed, even though it is the middle of the day."

I went off to my bedroom and laid down across my bed. Sunlight streamed through my winder. It was a long time before dark. And it seemed like a long time since I'd seen my room. It felt good to be back in it again, but somehow my rocks on the shelf and my peashooter and figures I'd carved out of wood looked like they belonged to someone else. I closed my eyes to see if I could feel like the old Arney Burdette. But I couldn't. I was all changed.

Chapter
26

"Inez Porter has been asking and asking about you." Ma's voice sounded like it come up out of a deep bog. I opened my eyes and she was there in my room looking down at me. "I told her everything that happened. She appears to be in mighty big awe of you and Sally. But . . . most especially of you. I reckon she'll be up here this evening wanting to hear all about it."

I opened my eyes. "What time is it, Ma?"

"Two o'clock . . . of the next day," Ma answered and I couldn't believe I'd slept all that long.

I looked up at the ceiling. Inez Porter . . . Inez . . . Seemed like I could almost feel that kiss she give me on my cheek that time. I raised my hand and touched my cheek. Then I closed my eyes and turned over with my back to Ma.

"I'm going to leave it up to you to tell Tice about his grandsons, Arnold," Ma said, and I whipped around and sat up in bed.

"Me? I don't want to tell him! I don't even want to *see* that mean old buzzard!"

"Tice needs to know and I've got Miz Doogle's dresses to finish for her and her girls to wear to her cousin's wedding over to Clement's Pond. I don't have the time to run over to his place. Besides, it should come from you."

I folded my fists and pounded them into the covers. *"I don't want to tell him!"* I yelled to the top of my lungs. "Let someone else tell him!"

"No one even wants to go around Tice after him not letting Amelia come home," Ma said with a sadness in her voice.

"Do you blame them?" I snarled.

Ma sighed. "Tice is caught up in bitterness of his own making. Ain't a day goes by that he don't hate hisself . . ."

"Or someone else!"

"Hisself more, Arnold. Much, much more. I reckon Tice has always put off on others his own shortcomings. If he could just like his own self, he'd see he'd like others better. And treat them better too. Now, Arnold, I want you to go down to his place and give him the news of his grandsons. Don't forget, it was *you* the Lord chose to save his life." Ma started to walk out and I called her back. Mad as I felt, I had to mention Sal's dress she wanted.

I started right in telling her how Sal had been longing for a dress for so long it was near about making her sick. "It's got to be prettier than anything you've ever made for Daphne Hazelton, Ma. It's got to be blue with a ruffle on the skirt and a collar made out of white lace and a velvet bow."

Ma looked down and said in a low voice, "I reckon I been too busy to notice how much Sally wants to have things."

"When can you make it, Ma?"

Ma pressed her lips together, rubbed her chin a little and blew a wisp of hair off her forehead. "I ain't going to make it, Arnold. I'm going to *buy* it. Jeb is going over to Tylersville tomorrow to get some things. I'm going to go with him and have him run me by The Trend Setter Shop. They'll have to have something close to the dress Sally wants."

"But how can you afford it, Ma?"

"I got a few dollars from selling eggs and from my sewing. I'll worry about the rest when the time comes." Ma come over to me then and leaned down to give me a hug. "Thank you for telling me about the dress, Arnold."

"Ma," I said, real stern, "I *still* don't want to go to old man Hooker's."

Ma let me go and moved back. "You *must*, Arnold!"

I scowled at the walls, at the ceiling, at the door Ma had just walked out of. Wasn't I never going to get shut of that old man? Looked like he was going to dog my tracks for the rest of my life! I throwed the covers back and jumped out of the bed and went over to the table where all my wood figures and peashooter and things was and give them all one good swipe right onto the floor. Dang that old man, anyway! He didn't deserve to know about Amelia and them babies! He didn't deserve anything but to be left alone by good folks and shunned by all the rest! I wished he'd dig a hole and fall down in it! I wished he'd dry up and blow away in the wind! *He* deserved to be dead and lost to the world! Not little Edward Morris.

I got dressed slow as I could. I didn't care how long it took me to get to old man Hooker's place. I didn't even

188

care if it took me a *month* to get there, but Ma was back at my door a little while later calling for me to hurry up and not be such a slowpoke.

"The sooner you get over there, the sooner Tice will know he is a gran'pa. You don't want to deprive a new gran'pa of knowing about his little grandson, do you?"

"Yes!" I shouted through the door.

"Cora," I heard Granny say, "you reckon you're being too hard on the boy by making him go over there?"

"This will help Arnold more than it will ever help Tice, Granny. That's why I'm sending him," Ma answered, and I could of spit a mile, I was so dang mad!

I throwed my coat on over my clothes and shoved my feet down into my boots so hard they hurt, then I opened the door and stomped all the way to the front door, out it, and down the steps. Buck and Bill come yapping up to me, jumping all around. "You might as well settle down," I told them. "I got to go to the devil's place and tell him about Amelia and them babies. But I ain't planning on staying there one minute after I get it all said." Buck and Bill follered me to the road, then turned around and ran back up to the house. I shoved my hands down deep into my coat pockets and started off, walking slow and easy, thinking I might even take a stroll around town, maybe go over and talk to Vesper Gene at the filling station or stop in the Cash-and-Carry and see what Mr. Doogle had new in the store, but my feet just kept on walking in the direction of old man Hooker's place.

When I finally reached the old man's shack, there was smoke roaring up out of the chimley like he was ready to set the place on fire again. The shack was all built back

189

now, thanks to my help, and looked better than it did before. Old man Hooker had even added an extry room to
put all his junk in. It would be a perfect room for Amelia,
Ma and Granny said, but he wouldn't let her have it, the
old coot! I took in a deep breath and went up to the door
and knocked on it.

"What you want?" Old man Hooker growled at me
through the door. He didn't even know it was me, but he'd
growl at anyone. I reckon he would of growled even *worse*
if he knowed it was me!

"It's Arney Burdette!" I growled back. "I got some news
for you!"

"I ain't innerested in no news!" he thundered. I expected
that.

"It's about Amelia!"

"What about Amelia?"

"She's give birth! She had two little boys . . ."

Before I could finish, the door snapped open and old
man Hooker stood there with his suspenders dropped off
his shoulders and hanging on each side of his hips. He had
on a raggedy gray undershirt and no shoes, as usual.

"Well, speak up!" he shouted at me.

"Amelia had her baby . . . *babies*. They was twin boys
and one died . . ."

"What do you mean, *one died?*" The old man shouted
fiercely and I stepped back. A peculiar look had come over
his face and I could see he was mighty affected by my
words.

"The one baby, he come breech and couldn't live," I
went on and told him everything as fast as I could, and he
hung on to every word I said, looking up suspiciously

190

through his eyebrows at me. When I come to the part about Amelia naming the baby after him his eyes got big and round.

"Where is Amelia?" he demanded.

"Still up on the mountain at Miz Simpson's cabin."

Suddenly he stepped back and slammed the door right in my face!

"Danged old fool!" I mumbled as I turned around and started stalking across the yard, kicking at every pebble and old rock that got in my way. "Ungrateful, dad-burned, stinking, nasty old hellion devil!" Behind me I heard the door snap open. I turned around and the old man was standing in the doorway.

"You tell your ma I need her to take me up to the mountain!" he shouted at me.

"No!" I blasted back at him. "I ain't telling Ma no such of a thing! You go find someone else to do for you! Ma and me has done all we're going to do for an ungrateful old buzzard like you!"

Old man Hooker glared at me like he was ready to run for me and kill me. But instead, he moved back and slammed the door. It banged so hard it sounded like thunder. I had to smile to myself, I was so glad I'd told the rotten old coot off. I turned around and was just walking by the old ramshackle barn when I seen Moonstruck Mulligan passing on the road with his gunnysack throwed across his shoulder and a neat, clean looking, long black coat buttoned up to his throat. Old man Hooker must of been looking out his winder and seen him at the same time because, all at once, the door whipped open and he called out to Moonstruck.

191

"Hightail it over to Lessie Fay's Boarding House and get someone to take me up the mountain! I got to see Amelia!" Moonstruck stopped and grinned and I snapped back behind the corner of the barn to listen. "Ain't no one going to take you nowheres," Moonstruck said. "You been too low-down mean to everyone, Tice Hooker. You must hate yourself right smart after all you done to folks."

Moonstruck and Ma was in agreement on that, all right. I braced myself for the cussing old man Hooker was going to give Moonstruck. But instead, he come out of the house and sunk down on the steps as loose as a dish rag and hung his head. Moonstruck entered the yard and went up to him. "You got to learn to temper your ways, Tice," he said, and old man Hooker looked up. His eyes was filled with tears and his old lips trembled over the words he spoke.

"What you say be t-true. I . . . I been so ornery, I reckon I . . . I don't know how to t-treat f-folks no . . . no more. I h-hated the world and everyone in it ever since . . . ever since the day my Ginny passed on and . . . and left me with Amelia to raise all alone."

It was hard to understand the old man's words, he was bawling so hard. My eyes and ears near about popped right out of my head when I realized what he was saying. I never expected to see the day Tice Hooker would admit to anyone what a mean old cuss he was. Suddenly he dropped his head into his hands and commenced to cry even harder. His thin old shoulders shook and his cries spread across the yard so heavy and loud that it sounded like his heart had split right in two.

"W-what good was I to Amelia? W-what good would I be to a . . . to a little baby?"

192

Moonstruck set his gunnysack on the ground and looked down at old man Hooker with that same expression he used to get when he preached in the church. "You can learn all the ways *not* to be the way you've been, brother. You been a fool stumbling around in the pit of darkness with your eyes closed. It's time you opened your eyes and let the light come in," he said over the old man's bellers. Then he took his juice harp out of his pocket and started in to play on it and to cut a jig right there.

It sure was a sight to see, old man Hooker slumped over and crying his eyes out and Moonstruck Mulligan playing on his juice harp with his feet flying and his shoulders looping all around like he was filled up to the brim and overflowing with spit and vinegar, and that long black coat whipping in all directions. But, I reckon for all of Moonstruck's strange ways, he had more truth than poetry in what he told old man Hooker.

While them two was occupied with their bawling and dancing, I scurried away from the barn and made a beeline for the road. I could still hear that old juice harp peppering out a tune in the cold air as I got further away from old man Hooker's place.

Chapter
27

After I'd been walking on the road awhile, a black Plymouth appeared in the distance, driving my way. It moved along slowly and, pretty soon, I could see that it was Miz Hazelton, and Daphne in the car with her. I thought about scampering off behind one of the trees alongside the road, but Daphne had already seen me. She was waving her hands out the car winder at me and her cheeks was all pushed up in a big smile.

The car slid along beside me and Daphne said out the winder, "Everybody is talking about you, Arney. I bet you're the most popular boy in all the county."

I looked down and scraped my brogans in the dirt. I reckon my face was plenty red. It felt like it would of burned my hand if I'd touched it. I looked up and said, "Don't leave Sal out of this."

"Oh . . . sure . . ." Daphne said, like she didn't care one thing about what Sal had done.

Miz Hazelton leaned her head down and looked across Daphne at me.

"Folks sure *is* talking about you and Sally. Mr. Parlier was just saying this morning when I seen him in the feed

194

store, that you and Sally has got more spunk than ten young'uns all stacked up in a row and Mr. Porter was telling Mr. Hazelton that you two ought to be a doctor and a nurse, the way you took care of Amelia." I reckoned word had spread mighty fast. I could feel my face getting red again. "Let me give you a ride home," Miz Hazelton went on.

"No, thanks, Miz Hazelton," I said.

"Oh, please, Arney," Daphne begged and her cheeks went down. "Mama will let us ride on the running boards, won't you, Mama?"

"Only if you promise to hang on good and not go to jumping off and on," Miz Hazelton answered with a smile.

"No . . . no, thanks," I said again, wishing they'd go on.

"Mama will drive slow, won't you, Mama," Daphne said.

"I always do," Miz Hazelton said with another smile.

I was beginning to feel a heavy pressure on me. Looked like Daphne and her Mama wasn't going to let up on me.

"Come on, Arney. It's fun."

"Well, all right," I said, and Daphne's face lit up and she opened the car door, got out and ran around to her mama's side and jumped up on the running board.

"Get on, Arney!" she called to me. I hopped up on the running board and hooked my hand around through the winder to hold on.

"Now, don't you young'uns jump off!" Miz Hazelton warned us and started up the car and we drove slowly down the road.

"Ain't this fun, Arney?" Daphne yelled across the roof of the car to me.

"Yeah!" I yelled back. But I reckoned I would of ruther

been anywhere than riding on the Hazelton's running board with Daphne. We continued along the road, going as slow as an old snail, with Daphne yelling and laughing things out at me like she was as happy as could be.

"Hang on now," Miz Hazelton called when she made the turn into my yard.

Daphne hung onto the winder with both hands and let the turn blow her way out like she was a flag in the wind. She was laughing and carrying on and yelling WHEEEEEEEE! all the time the car was turning. I was glad when Miz Hazelton stopped the car and I could jump off the running board. Buck and Bill was already barking and jumping around and, over it all, I could hear Daphne begging her mama to let her stay the rest of the day. I bent down and went to scratching Bill's ears, to hide my face.

"I ain't heard no invite, child," Miz Hazelton said.

"You want me to stay, don't you, Arney?" Daphne asked, and she leaped off the running board and come flying around the car to me.

I swallered and gulped and cleared my throat. "Well . . ." is all I could get out before Sal come out on the front porch and Daphne took off running up the steps, calling out, "Mama says I can stay the whole day with you and Arney, Sally!"

Sal flashed her eyes up and down the pretty coat Daphne had on and bit into her lip. Just then the Porter's car come pulling into the yard. I looked up and seen Inez setting between her mama and daddy and my heart commenced to zing like plucked guitar strings! Daphne looked around and said with a sneer of disappointment, "Oh . . . it's *Inez*."

196

"Inez has come to spend the afternoon with me, Daphne. So . . . well, I reckon you can't stay," Sal said with a lift of her chin.

Daphne's face fell. She give Sal a narrow eyed look, muttered something I couldn't hear and took off down the steps to her mama's car. When she got the door closed, she looked out at me and said, "Maybe I'll come and see you tomorrow, Arney."

As Miz Hazelton pulled away she and the Porters passed a greeting from the cars, then she drove on off the place onto the road. Daphne's head was still hanging out of the car winder with that disappointed look on her face.

"If you ain't all I ever seen, I don't know what is!" Mr. Porter's voice floated over my shoulder, and I looked around. "You keep on with all them good deeds and we'll have to send you up to Washington to take over for the President!"

"Now, Hyram, we wouldn't do a thing like that. Not even if we could," Miz Porter said, turning to her husband and speaking loud enough for me to hear. "We're going to keep Arnold right here in Weedpatch. No telling what a boy like him will be able to do for a town like this someday."

It sure was a day for me to turn red! My face felt like a brush fire had broke out on it. The Porters was always going on with each other like that. They was kind and amusing and both of them was tall and skinny as bean poles. I reckon, since Inez was so pretty, she got the best out of each one of them.

Mr. Porter turned to Inez setting between him and Miz Porter. "Well, I reckon you want out of here. It'll cost you

197

a penny." Then he said to me, "You got a penny to let this here gal out of the car, Arnold?"

My face turned redder than a garden full of beets and Mr. Porter laughed.

"Now, Hyram, quit your playing," Miz Porter said, and Mr. Porter got out of the car and let Inez out. "We'll be back to get you just before supper, Inez honey," Miz Porter called after Inez as she ran up the porch steps.

After the Porters drove away from the house, Inez come back down the steps and walked up to me. Sal turned and went inside the house. I didn't have much of a chance to wonder why because my heart had started playing on them guitar strings again and it was hard to get hold of my breath. My eyes ran all the way down through them blond curls and brown eyes, past her dark gray coat with the great big round gray buttons on it, to her shoes and back up to meet her smile. Before either one of us could say a word, Buck and Bill beat a path to us and started jumping up at us. Inez bent down to pet Bill and I bent down to rub old Buck's neck and they settled down. Me and Inez stared at each other over their long, skinny reddish-brown backs.

"Do you want to go for a walk, Inez?" I asked. But after I said it, I wondered if I should of. I knowed Inez had come to visit with Sal.

"I'd like to," Inez answered with a smile. We stood up and Buck and Bill took off in a race to the house.

"Do you reckon you ought to tell Sal?" I asked. "I mean, she might be disappointed that you ain't with her."

"She won't be. Me and Sal planned it this way." I had to blink my eyes hard at that! "I'll be with you a little. Then I'll be with Sally a little." Her smile got even bigger, like her and Sal had some kind of secret.

198

We walked out of the yard and along the road and I shoved my hands down into my coat pockets. "Are you cold?" I asked her.

"No," she said, and I looked down to watch my brogans make prints in the damp, soft ground. I could feel her eyes on me and I looked up at her. "Oh, Arney, I'm so proud to know you and Sally. You're both so brave to of done what you did. I was proud of you when you saved Tice Hooker's life and . . ."

"I didn't want to save his life! Not no time! Ever!" Them words flew out fast and hard, before I could even think to stop them.

"But you did. Even if you didn't want to."

"My heart was all wrong."

"Your heart was all *right*, Arney, else you never would of saved him. And you ain't never going to make me believe you're anything but the bravest, nicest, and best boy I've ever knowed."

My heart commenced to ache in a strange way. I never expected to hear Inez Porter talk to me like that! We walked a little bit more and I inched closer to her and, next thing, my arm had shot out real quick and curled around her waist. Then her head come down on my shoulder and them blond curls went to tickling against my neck. I reckoned I would lean down and kiss her real good, just like I'd seen them actors in the movies do. They was one feller by the name of Charles Bow something-or-other that knowed how to do it real well. I seen him lots of times. Only thing was, he didn't seem nervous at all. I took in a deep breath and moved my head a little, and Inez snapped her head around at the same time and our noses met in a hard crash.

"Oh!" Inez squealed and put her hand over her nose. "Are you hurt real bad?" I asked, feeling like a fool. Some Charles whatever-his-name I was!

Inez laughed and at the same time it commenced to rain so hard we had to take off our coats and hold them over our heads as we ran back to the house. When we reached the porch, Inez took her coat off her head and come up to me and give me a little peck right on my lips. Then she ran in the house calling out for Sal. Her kiss was as wet as the rain and I wished I could pour it in a jar and keep it forever.

Chapter

28

When Ma come home from visiting the Crimps and their new baby, she told how Jeb had took old man Hooker up to the mountain to get Amelia. He was going to bring her back to live with him.

"Praise the Lord!" Granny near about shouted. Then in a thoughtful voice she said, "Ain't it strange how that old man will act sometimes."

"You mean, Granny, 'ain't it strange' how old man Hooker acts *all* the time!" I spoke up.

"Now, Arnold," Ma said from over at the sink where she was making coffee. "Don't keep holding a grudge. Time will pass and you'll soften in your feelings. *If* you allow yourself to."

"No, I won't! I won't never!" I said. But I'd already given up on killing the old fool. Seemed like, much as I wanted to do it, my insides wouldn't let me. And when such thoughts overtook me, they'd soon be swept away by thoughts of little Edward Morris laying in that drawer in Reba Simpson's cabin. I'd get hot all over again. But I'd cool down too.

"A feller has to forgive seven times seventy and make up his mind to be satisfied, no matter what," Granny said with a loud smack of her lips. Ma turned away from the sink and give Granny a long look. Then she set the coffee pot on the stove and come up to Granny where we was both setting at the table and give Granny a hug. "You know you'll always have a home with us, Granny," she said. I reckon we both knowed that Granny was thinking about her little home she had to give up because of old man Hooker.

Granny patted Ma on her arm and said, "I can't wait for spring when I can get outside and into planting some snap beans and tomaters and flowers and work around in the sun." It sure was something the way Granny could forgive Tice Hooker and look to the future.

News spread all around about old man Hooker taking Amelia and the baby in and how he made peace with her. I couldn't believe it at first, but I reckoned it was true because a week or so after him and Jeb brought her and the baby down from the mountain, he actually come to church wearing new shoes and a new suit of clothes. I reckon Amelia made him clean hisself up. It sure set folks to buzzing and poking each other and straining their necks to get a gander at him.

But old man Hooker wasn't the only one with a new set of clothes. Ma was so proud of Sal she found a dress for Sal that was even prettier than the one she had described to me that she wanted. It was blue, all right, and had a white lace collar with a tiny black velvet bow tie in the center of it and the skirt didn't have *one* ruffle. It had *three*. As soon as Sal pulled it up out of the box and the white tissue paper fell away from it, she hugged it to her and cried with her eyes squeezed closed, "Oh! It's sooo beautiful! It's just the kind of dress I always wanted!"

But that wasn't all Sal got. Ma had got her a shiny black pair of patent leather shoes and a white straw hat with a long blue satin ribbon to tie under her chin. It made a lump come into my throat to see her looking so pretty. She looked so good, she put Daphne Hazelton right to shame! You could tell Daphne was plumb put out over Sal's new clothes and her looking so good in them. I reckoned Travis and Gussie thought she looked good too. Their eyes stayed glued to her all the time Preacher Jessup was up at the pulpit shouting out praises to the Lord.

That first Sunday after old man Hooker come to church, Ma invited him and Amelia and the baby to supper at our house. Me and Sal give each other a disgusted look when she told us about the company we was going to have. "Why did you have to invite *him*?" I wanted to know. I was beginning to think I'd got shut of him once and for all.

"So Tice can tell you something special," Ma answered me, and me and Sal give each other another look.

Sal and Granny set the table and Ma fixed up a pot of chicken and dumplings and greens and hot cornbread and apple pies that near about set my belly to singing. I didn't like it much, though, that Ma went so all out for old man Hooker. It was different with Amelia. I reckoned she deserved special treatment after what she'd been through.

When we was all setting at the table old man Hooker acted like he couldn't hardly look at me. I'd look up from my plate and catch him staring at me and, soon as he seen my eyes on him, he'd look away. I reckoned the old fool knowed how I felt about him, all right. When I was ready to say grace, he reached out and grabbed for a slice of corn bread and Amelia cut right into him.

"Now, Daddy, it's time you minded your manners. You wouldn't want little Arnold Tice to take up impolite ways, now would you?"

I stared at Amelia like I hadn't heard her right. She had the baby in her arms at the table and was smiling at me. I glanced around. Ma and Granny and Sal was smiling at me too. I looked around at old man Hooker and his face was full of red polka dots. He was running his finger along the inside of his shirt collar and looking everywhere but at me.

"Go on, Daddy. Tell Arnold," Amelia said, and old man Hooker grunted and looked up at me under his eyebrows, then down again real fast. "Go on, Daddy," Amelia said again.

"Errrr . . . ahhhh . . . arrr . . ." old man Hooker stuttered. It was the first time I ever seen him at a loss for words. I glanced at Sal. She looked like she was ready to go to laughing. "Well, we . . . ah . . . we named the baby Arnold."

"Daddy!" Amelia said sternly.

"*I* named the baby Arnold!" The old fool blasted out across the table like he was so mad at me he could of jumped up and knocked me right out of my chair. I couldn't do a thing but stare.

"And what else, Daddy?" Amelia asked.

"I got an old turkey give to me. If you . . . if you and your sister want the damned thing, you can have it!" he blasted out again like he wished he could grab me around my neck and throw me onto the floor and beat my brains right out of my head! I reckon it took every bit of power the old man had in him to say them things.

"Well, Lord bless you!" Granny said.

"Humph!" old man Hooker grunted.

"What do you have to say, Arnold?" Ma asked, and I wished she hadn't asked me a thing. I was too stunned to even open my mouth.

"Arnold don't have to say anything. I just hope my little son grows up to be as fine a boy as he is," Amelia said, smiling at me.

"Thank you, dear," Ma said, and she give me a smile too.

When supper was over and Ma went to drive Amelia and old man Hooker home, Granny said to me, "Think of all the honors you been getting, Arnold."

"What are you talking about, Granny?" I asked her with a frown.

"Why, the Lord intrusted you to save Tice Hooker twice . . ."

Three times, I corrected her in my mind. But I didn't say anything. I just let her go on talking.

"And now he's give Amelia's baby your name." Granny took off her glasses and wiped the corner of her apron over them.

I studied Granny close, remembering what she had told me and Sal about her little house that old man Hooker tossed her out of. With all the good things happening, I wondered if someday the old fool might soften enough to let her move back into it.

Chapter
29

That night, out on the porch, me and Sal was watching the fireflies flit around in the darkness and listening to the steady "chip, chip, chip" sound the crickets made up close to the house. The night was cool with the smell of spring on its way and the feel of our sweaters was all we needed. Off in the distance we could hear one of Jeb's cows and off beyond that, the sound of the train rattling past Weedpatch with its whistle shouting out. It never stopped in Weedpatch. It always went on by and stopped in Clement's Pond.

"What we going to call the turkey, Arney?" Sal asked after the train had went on by.

"I don't know," I answered. "All I know is, it was that mean old man that killed Gobble and I'll never forget it."

"I reckon he's trying to make it up to us."

"Well, he can't."

Sal sighed. "I think I'll call him 'Gobble Esquire.' "

I snickered. "How come that?"

"Because Gobble was a knight. A knight with beautiful feathers that was his shining armor. An 'esquire' always comes after a knight. Miz Tinker said so."

Sal sure was something. I reckoned before long, she'd be making up a song about that old Gobble being a knight in King Arthur's Court or something. We was studying about it in school.

"I'm going to make a special place for Gobble Esquire in the yard near Ma's flower bed where they is plenty of worms for him to eat," Sal went on.

"I reckon Gobble Esquire would like that," I said, and I looked out at the road. A lone figure was passing in the darkness. "Who you reckon that is?" I asked Sal.

"I don't know," Sal said, squinting her eyes into the darkness.

I leaned forward and peered hard at the figure. Then I seen the long coat whipping around his legs as he walked and the gunnysack tossed over his shoulder and I knowed it was Moonstruck Mulligan. I stood up and cupped my hands over my mouth and yelled out, "Where you going, Moonstruck?"

He looked around and stopped. "Off to Glory," he called back.

Me and Sal snickered. "Well, don't get lost!" I yelled.

"Can't get lost, boy! This road is straight and narrow and I done passed all the detours. Can't go no other way but straight." He took off walking again, and me and Sal watched him until he disappeared into the shadders.

"You reckon old Moonstruck is as crazy as everyone says?" Sal asked as I sat down.

Just then we heard the music from Moonstruck's juice harp. It filled up the night and give it a special sweetness. I leaned back on the porch and rested on my arm. "No," I said. "I don't reckon he is."